"I'm Not Letting You Go."

Jack turned Lizzie toward the sea and held on to her from behind. "If you fall in, then I'll have to go get you. And, babe, I'm thinking that would be a bad idea. Rule One, stay on the boat."

"I told you, I'm not a babe."

"And I'm not Ahab."

"It's either that or Captain Hook, since we seem to be following a fairy-tale theme."

"Both my hands are intact." Definitely so, because they'd somehow made their way to her hips.

"I guess you're right about that, so Ahab it is."

He couldn't hold back a smile. "Are you feeling better now?"

Lizzie drew in a deep breath. "I just need something to eat."

Jack needed to kiss her, badly.

Dear Reader,

Top off your summer reading list with six brand-new steamy romances from Silhouette Desire!

Reader favorite Ann Major brings the glamorous LONE STAR COUNTRY CLUB miniseries into Desire with *Shameless* (#1513). This rancher's reunion romance is the first of three titles set in Mission Creek, Texas—where society reigns supreme and appearances are everything. Next, our exciting yearlong series DYNASTIES: THE BARONES continues with *Beauty & the Blue Angel* (#1514) by Maureen Child, in which a dashing naval hero goes overboard for a struggling mom-to-be.

Princess in His Bed (#1515) by *USA TODAY* bestselling author Leanne Banks is the third Desire title in her popular miniseries THE ROYAL DUMONTS. Enjoy the fun as a tough Wyoming rancher loses his heart to a spirited royal-in-disguise. Next, a brooding horseman shows a beautiful rancher the ropes...of desire in *The Gentrys: Abby* (#1516) by Linda Conrad.

In the latest BABY BANK title, *Marooned with a Millionaire* (#1517) by Kristi Gold, passion ignites between a powerful hotel magnate and the pregnant balloonist stranded on his yacht. And a millionaire M.D. brings out the temptress in his tough-girl bodyguard in *Sleeping with the Playboy* (#1518) by veteran Harlequin Historicals and debut Desire author Julianne MacLean.

Get your summer off to a sizzling start with six new passionate, powerful and provocative love stories from Silhouette Desire.

Enjoy!

Melissa Jeglinski
Senior Editor, Silhouette Desire

Please address questions and book requests to:
Silhouette Reader Service
U.S.: 3010 Walden Ave., P.O. Box 1325, Buffalo, NY 14269
Canadian: P.O. Box 609, Fort Erie, Ont. L2A 5X3

Marooned with a Millionaire

KRISTI GOLD

Published by Silhouette Books

America's Publisher of Contemporary Romance

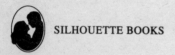

SILHOUETTE BOOKS

ISBN 0-373-76517-7

MAROONED WITH A MILLIONAIRE

Visit Silhouette at www.eHarlequin.com

Printed in U.S.A.

KRISTI GOLD

has always believed that love has remarkable healing powers and feels very fortunate to be able to weave stories of romance and commitment. As a bestselling author and Romance Writers of America RITA® Award finalist, she's learned that although accolades are wonderful, the most cherished rewards come from the most unexpected places, namely from personal stories shared by readers. Kristi resides on a ranch in Central Texas with her husband and three children, along with various and sundry livestock. She loves to hear from readers and can be contacted at KGOLDAUTHOR@aol.com or P.O. Box 11292, Robinson, TX 76716.

To Captain Jeremy and First Mate Pattie, for all the wonderful insight and nautical details you've provided during the making of this story. Here's wishing you both another twenty-five years of smooth sailing.

One

The sailboat's sudden pitch jarred Jackson Dunlap from his solitude and sent the mug before him into his lap. Bolting from his seat in the galley, he scaled the companionway leading topside at a sprint, covered in coffee and cursing the sudden commotion.

For one solid year, not much had disturbed him as he'd sailed alone off the coast of Florida. At his request, he'd had no visitors, no business calls, no disruptions aside from the necessary returns to port to restock and the occasional patch of rough weather. Until now.

After arriving on deck, Jack shaded his eyes against the midday June sun expecting to find he'd been rammed by some craft piloted by an idiot or a nearsighted whale in the throes of mating season. He didn't expect to see the patchwork purple-and-yellow balloon slowly descending from the sky and deflating not more than a few hundred yards away.

He moved closer to the sight, unable to comprehend what he now witnessed. Some guy in the gondola attached to the balloon was waving like mad until the basket bounced along the surface, toppled, then spilled its human contents.

Spurred into action by a surge of adrenaline and a sudden sense of déjà vu, Jack raced to the platform at the stern. ''Swim!'' he yelled as he tossed a buoy in the general direction of the stranger, thankful he'd lowered the sails that morning. At least the boat was somewhat stationary. And luckily the current seemed to be aiding the guy in his efforts. Unfortunately, it was also aiding the balloon and basket to travel in the same direction, toward his prized boat.

Jack feverishly tugged the buoy's line, dragging the stranger through the water at a fast clip. Then suddenly he realized he wasn't a he at all. He was a she. A woman with wide oval eyes and chin-length blond hair that hung down around her face in wet strands.

What the hell was she doing all the way out here?

He planned to ask her that—and more—as soon as he had her safely on board.

Once she was within reach, Jack grabbed her extended arm, tugged her onto the platform, tossed her over his shoulder and headed forward.

''I can walk,'' she said in a raspy, winded voice. ''So you can put me down now.''

He could, but not until he made sure she wasn't injured. Gingerly he laid her on the deck and sat beside her, uncertain which one of them was breathing more heavily. His ragged respiration had more to do with nerves than exertion because she really didn't weigh all that much. He imagined her labored breath resulted from the swim along with a little added fear—and rightfully so.

When he regained his voice, he asked, "Are you hurt?"

She scooted into a sitting position and stared at him with blue-green eyes almost a perfect match to the sea. Then she opened her mouth and muttered, "I'm okay as long as the baby's okay."

Baby? She had a kid with her? "Was the baby in the basket?" he asked in a moderate tone, struggling to keep the panic from his voice.

She studied him with sandy brows drawn down over confused eyes. Then she laid a hand on her belly and smiled. "It's in this basket."

Both relieved and shocked, his gaze shot to her slender hand now curved protectively over her abdomen. "You're pregnant?"

She pushed her damp hair away from her forehead and exhaled slowly. "Yes."

Great. Just great.

"Are you sure you're feeling all right?" he asked, genuinely concerned. "No pain or anything?"

She sat a little straighter. "I'm okay. Kind of tired, but overall pretty good."

Jack decided she looked pretty good all over. Healthy, he corrected. Her still-flat abdomen encased in plain white capri pants, the soaked yellow T-shirt adhering to her torso, made Jack hard-pressed to believe she was actually going to have a baby.

Obviously she wasn't very far along in the pregnancy. Obviously she couldn't lay claim to much common sense, either, which made him *really* want to shake some sense into her. But she'd been shaken up enough for one day, so he settled for a little subtle chastising. "Now let me see if I've got this straight. You decided to go off in your balloon to tour the ocean at the risk of harming your unborn child?"

She hugged her knees to her chest and glared at him. "For your information, ballooning is a very safe mode of transportation. I'm more at risk driving on a Miami freeway. I would never do anything, *anything*, to hurt my baby. This was a fluke."

A bite of guilt nipped at Jack. He had no call to judge anyone when it came to taking risks. God knew he had taken more than his share, with much more devastating consequences.

He sent her a half smile, a feeble attempt at an apology. "I suppose it's a lot like sailing. Once it's in the blood, you can't consider giving it up."

She glanced away but not before he caught a hint of sadness in her eyes. "Actually, it was my last trip until after the baby's birth. I was leaving a festival near Miami. I'm not sure what happened. I think I might have passed out or something. The next thing I knew, I woke up out here, wherever here is."

"We're about twenty miles off the coast near Key Largo. You couldn't get back to shore?"

"By the time I came to, the wind was unstable and I started losing altitude."

He supposed that made sense, as much sense as it could to a man who preferred water to air. Sometimes the elements couldn't be controlled. How well he knew that concept.

She gave him a sheepish smile, revealing a glimpse of white teeth and a dimple at the left corner of her lower lip. "Pretty lucky I happened upon you, huh?"

That remained to be seen, Jack decided. "Did you hit the deck when you were trying to land?"

"Not exactly."

"It sounded like you hit something."

"More like grazed."

"The deck?"

She pointed upward. "The mast thingy. I aimed for it on my descent. I wanted to make sure I got your attention."

It had definitely gotten his attention, then and now. And admittedly a smart thing for her to do, not that he cared for it much. No telling what kind of damage she'd done, but at least she hadn't brought the mast down. At the moment he didn't dare examine the *thingy*, fearing what he might find. Right now he was barely hanging on to some semblance of calm. Right now he had to deal with another pressing matter.

Coming to his feet, he asked with a great deal of benevolence, "Are you sure you're okay?"

"I'm fine. Really. Promise."

"Okay. I'm going to go see where the balloon went. I'll be right back. You rest."

Her expression reflected gratitude. "Thanks. I'd appreciate that."

He decided not to tell her that his concern was for his boat, not her balloon. And he hoped like hell the damn thing had changed course.

But it hadn't. He realized that the moment he arrived at the rear platform. The massive fabric billowed portside; the basket was lodged on the end of the swim ladder.

Tethering himself to the platform railing, he lowered to his stomach and inched down until he could reach the rig. With the set of bolt cutters stored aft, he started to work. First he dislodged the gondola and began cutting away the cables attaching the balloon to the framework that housed the burner. He fought the current's pull, fought the sea spray jetting into his face. Fought his desperation and impatience. He continued practically blind but knew he was making progress when the fabric began pulling away.

Finally, the last cable snapped. His fingers ached, his eyes burned, but he supposed he should feel lucky that the rig hadn't made its way underneath the boat. That could mean certain disaster.

"What are you doing?"

He hadn't realized she was standing behind him. Right behind him. Without looking at her, he said, "I've freed your balloon." Gave it a nice burial at sea, he almost told her but thought better of it.

"Why did you do that?"

"So it didn't get caught up in the prop."

Standing, he turned to face her and met the most melancholy expression he'd ever seen on a woman's face. He couldn't really blame her. He'd felt the same way when he'd lost his last boat to a cutthroat competition coupled with a relentless storm. He'd lost more than that.

At least he had saved her. At least she was alive, unharmed, in charge of all her faculties....

"Can you go get the envelope...the balloon itself? We could roll it up and store it on deck."

Obviously she was crazy. Certifiable. "Not unless you expect me to swim for it."

She wrapped her arms around her middle as she visually followed the flattened balloon now barely perceptible on the horizon. "Of course, that's a stupid thing to ask considering what you've done for me. But that balloon is my livelihood."

When this ordeal ended, he'd buy her another balloon. Hell, he had enough money to buy her fifty balloons, not that he had any desire to tell her that. The less she knew about him, the better. "I'm sorry, but I had no choice."

She gave him a one-shoulder shrug and a surprisingly bright grin. "I'm sure it will all work out somehow. I'll think of something."

Great. A blond optimist, Jack thought. A tall, blond optimist, not without some fairly liberal curves that were more than obvious beneath her clinging clothing. Admittedly, she was pretty darned cute, even if she was a little scattered. Scattered and sexy. She was also shaking.

Turning his back on all that cuteness, he said, "Follow me. Let's get you out of your clothes." *Oh, hell.* "You can wear some of mine."

Without protest she complied, and once they'd made it into the main salon, he faced her again. "It's a little warmer in here. That should help.'' Not Jack, though. He was already way too hot under the collar.

"Thanks,'' she murmured. "I owe you.''

He considered one form of payment that would not be at all appropriate, or advisable. He had no use for women, cute or otherwise. Especially a woman who had interrupted his nice solitary life. A pregnant woman, no less. More than likely a married pregnant woman.

Something suddenly occurred to Jack, something he should have considered long before now. "After you change, we can try to get a message to your husband.''

She executed a prideful tip of her chin. "That would be futile since I don't have one.''

"Boyfriend?'' Jack asked, more than slightly curious, regardless of his caution.

She shook her head. "Nope.''

"Miraculous conception?''

Strolling to the navy-and-red plaid sofa, she ran her fingers along the edge. "If you're inquiring about the father of my child, he's not involved.''

And it was really none of Jack's business. He sure as hell didn't want her in the middle of his. "Okay. What about friends and family?''

"Actually, the members of my chase crew are probably wondering what happened to me when they saw me drift away.''

"I'm sure they are.'' And Jack wondered what was happening to him. He couldn't stop looking at her now exposed earlobe, her nice full mouth, her long, slender limbs—and imagining things he had no cause to imagine. For God's sake, he didn't even know her name.

With that in mind, he stuck out his hand. "Jackson Dunlap. I prefer Jack."

Her grin illuminated the dimly lit cabin as she took his hand. "Elizabeth Matheson, and I prefer another name altogether. However, you may call me Lizzie."

Despite his need to remain detached, he couldn't suppress his own smile. "Well, Lizzie, at least we have a few things settled."

Unfortunately, he felt very unsettled. As crazy as it seemed, the woman glowed, even when she wasn't smiling. Even soaking wet and shivering, she possessed a weird kind of aura that would make most men take immediate notice. He certainly had. He was still noticing.

He didn't have time to notice. He had to check out the mainsail and mast, and get the hell back to port.

Chalking up his disregard for his boat to months of celibacy, he simply said, "Bathroom's in there, if you want to use it." He pointed to the starboard head.

Her gaze swept the room and her smile returned. "Fantastic boat. It's probably bigger than my apartment. Who owns it?"

"I do."

"Oh. So where's the rest of the crew?"

Long lost to the sea, Jack thought with the same old remorse. "It's only me. I prefer it that way."

She continued to survey the area. "Really? You handle this baby all by yourself? I'm impressed."

So was he. Too impressed. With her. "You go

grab a shower, I'll go grab you some clothes.'' And he would do his best not to grab her for the few remaining hours they would spend together.

With a nervous twist of her hands and another luminous smile, she said, ''Okay,'' then walked toward the head while regarding him over one shoulder. ''You might want to bring me just a T-shirt since I doubt I could get into your shorts.''

He'd be willing to let her try.

Jack's reaction to her innocent, offhand comment and the image it produced created a not-so-nonchalant response down south. ''Fine. A T-shirt it is. Take your time. I'll get things moving so we can head for land.''

The quicker he got rid of her, the better, for the sake of his own sanity and his valued seclusion.

Jackson Carter Dunlap, hotel magnate and self-made millionaire, didn't like the thought of anyone disrupting the way of life he had come to know over the past twelve months. But damned if the woman who'd fallen from the sky like some misguided Dorothy wasn't driving him to distraction. And it had taken her all of twelve minutes.

If Lizzie never tasted salt again, it would be too soon. At least the accommodations were first-rate, she thought as she sank farther into the garden tub, immersing herself in the warmth of fresh water.

The bathroom was much bigger than she'd envisioned, but it made sense. A big bathroom for one big strappin' guy with broad shoulders and large hands. Except he had narrow hips, something she'd noticed immediately while walking behind him, shamelessly scrutinizing his butt.

She had also noticed his silver eyes because he'd had them trained on her from the beginning. Rugged was the first thought that had come to mind when she'd gotten a good look at him. His brown hair, sun-bleached on the ends, gave him a totally natural look. A good thing because she'd never gone for the kind of guy who got his highlights from a bottle. Mr. Dunlap wasn't that kind at all. In fact, she couldn't imagine him sitting still for a dye job, or sitting still for very long, period. She really liked his face, his healthy-looking skin. Nice and tan. But before he ruined it, someone really ought to remind him of the dangers of prolonged UV exposure. Maybe she would. Maybe she'd better not.

Although he could use a little cleanup, a shave and haircut, Lizzie got the definite impression that beneath Jack Dunlap's added fur there existed some interesting territory many a woman would like to explore. But not her. Of course, not her. Being the plain sort, not at all a bombshell blonde, she wasn't really any man's ideal, and for the most part she'd been fine with that.

Oh, she had lots of men friends, but very few that had viewed her as a romantic prospect. Only one man, in fact. That relationship had happened a long time ago, without great success. Nothing tragic, no broken hearts. Just plain old apathy on the part of both parties. Recently she hadn't met one guy that she'd cared to try on for size.

Not that Jack Dunlap hadn't jump-started a few of

her fantasies. But her host was just a tad bit irritated by her presence even though he had been accommodating. She'd sensed that immediately after he'd verified for himself she wasn't hurt. Thank the Lord she hadn't been hurt.

Resting her palm on her tummy, she smiled with relief. "Well, little Hank, Mommy almost did a number on us this time. But I promise, from now on, I'll take good care of you. No more balloon flights until after you're born. Heck, if I ever get off this boat, I might never do anything more risky than jaywalk, as long as there's no oncoming traffic."

Considering she no longer had a balloon, that wouldn't be a problem. This meant she no longer had a balloon business, either. She couldn't afford to buy another even though she would receive some insurance money. But it wouldn't be enough to replace it, or to pay her crew and a pilot to take over for her until after the baby was born.

She only had limited savings left from her father's life insurance, and that was for the baby. The rest she had used to keep the business going, the business her dad had always dreamed of owning. A dream he had never achieved.

Hank Matheson, her beloved father, had raised Lizzie by himself since the year she'd turned four—the same year her mother had died. He'd taught her how to fly. He'd taught her a lot, the most important being that life was what you made it. No matter how tough things got, silver linings did exist. Lizzie still believed that and probably always would, even if she didn't have a job at present.

She supposed she could go back to being Lizzie the Makeover Artist at the salon. Less stress than owning her own business. Less money, too.

Lizzie toyed with the necklace at her throat. The chain contained her two most prized possessions—her father's St. Christopher medal and the heart he had given her mother on their first anniversary, four months before Lizzie's birth. Her good-luck charms served as a reminder that everything would work out, as it always had. After all, she'd survived losing her only family. She would survive this loss, too, because in the end, she wouldn't be alone. She would have her baby.

A grinding sound followed by a loud curse pulled Lizzie out of her musings. Obviously Ahab was in command of some colorful language, even a few compound words she hadn't heard except on cable-TV comedy shows.

Maybe she should just submerse herself underwater until he calmed down from whatever had him so irate. Maybe she was responsible for his rant.

The door flew open and the man with many curses entered the room. "Here's your T-shirt." He tossed it onto the cabinet where she'd laid out her clothes and underwear to dry.

Covered only by clear water and a full-body blush, she attempted to look pleasant. "This tub is heavenly."

"It's also full of water."

He not only cussed like a typical sailor, he also talked in codes. "Yes. That's what you usually do. Fill it up."

He scowled. "I have limited fresh water on board. We have to be conservative."

He moved closer to the edge of the tub, and Lizzie decided then and there that if he hadn't seen her in the altogether when he'd entered the room, he certainly could now. What the heck. She couldn't really cover herself, and frankly she wasn't all that inhibited when it came to her body. However, the smoldering look in his eyes made her want to roll over onto her belly, face down, to try to rid herself of the heat his presence had generated.

Instead, she came to her knees, folded her arms on the tub's ledge and rested her chin atop them. "I would really like some privacy, if you don't mind."

"I've seen a naked woman before."

"Not this naked woman."

His gaze slid over her once more. "I'm not looking."

Could've fooled her. "Thanks for the T-shirt. Is there anything else?"

He turned toward the cabinet and studied her undies. Guess he didn't find her drawers at all satisfactory. Obviously he resented her cluttering his bathroom. Or he might just plain resent her.

"Actually, there is something else," he said. "Several things. First, the rules about bathing on the boat."

"I promise I won't take another bath while I'm here."

"I doubt that."

"Seriously, Jack, I don't bathe twice a day unless I happen to exert myself."

That brought his attention back to her. "It's going to take us more than a day to get back to land."

"I didn't think we were that far offshore."

"Relatively speaking, we're not. But we have a few problems."

From the stony look on his face, Lizzie wasn't sure she wanted to hear about their problems. But she guessed she might as well. "What's wrong?"

He rolled his neck on his shoulders, obviously dealing with a pain perhaps directly associated with her. "First of all, I went to check on the mast, to see if you did any damage. When I raised the sail, it blew out. The jib might catch some wind, if there was any, but there's not much to speak of. And to top it off, the sails won't come down because the block was damaged when you hit the mast."

"Oh." It was all she could think to say. "Surely the Coast Guard will be here soon."

"Not likely."

"Didn't you call them?"

"I tried. Your little basket took out the radio antenna."

She frowned. "Oh, so that's what that was."

"Yeah, that's what that was. I have no way to communicate with anyone."

Surely things weren't as dire as he had made them out to be. "Doesn't this boat have some sort of an engine?"

"Under normal circumstances, yes. But I have no power since something's caught up on the prop. Would you happen to know what that could be?"

"You did cut the cables, right?"

"Yeah."

"What about the tether lines?"

"Tether lines?"

Uh-oh. "The ones that hang from the gondola. They tie down the balloon once you're grounded."

His scowl made her want to shrivel and shrink. "Great. Thanks for telling me." He turned toward the door but before exiting faced her again. "Take your time, princess. Might be your last soak for a long while."

The nerve of him, calling her princess. Nobody called her that and got away with it. She stood without regard to her nudity. "I'm quite through now, and I'm definitely not a princess." *Ahab.*

His silver eyes darkened as he gave her a lingering once-over, from chin to thighs, pausing at intimate places in between. "I could argue that point, but right now I have other things to do."

Then he was gone, leaving her dripping, naked and totally bumfuzzled. Full of questions she needed answered now, whether he liked it or not.

Princess. Ha! She'd just have to show him that when backed into a corner, Queen Elizabeth could be a royal pain in the posterior.

Two

Lizzie grabbed the towel hanging from the bar at the end of the tub and quickly dried. She shoved the T-shirt over her head, thankful it was long enough to provide adequate cover. Refusing to wear soggy panties, she stomped out of the bathroom, barefoot and covered only in thin cotton. If she hadn't lost her canvas slides during the swim, then she could give Ahab a swift kick in his great-looking butt for good measure.

As she left the bathroom in search of the salty seadog, she tried to tell herself that she understood his frustration, his snippy attitude. He'd been minding his own business, bothering no one, until she'd dropped in unannounced. But did he really have to be so nasty? She couldn't help that he'd been the only thing in sight when she'd made her emergency landing. And a nice landing it was, even if he didn't appreciate it. After all, she could've landed on his precious deck and swamped the entire boat, then where would he be? Quite possibly on the bottom of the ocean, and so would she.

She searched the living area but didn't find him anywhere. When she started for the closed door at the rear of the boat, the sound of footsteps above drew her up the steps. By Bess, he was going to talk to her even if she had to sit on him. Now that might be fun.

Naughty, naughty girl, Lizzie, she silently scolded as she strode to her destination with wavering purpose, a little nervous over the prospect of facing his wrath. But that would not deter her. When she surfaced on the deck, she noticed the sun had all but set, providing just enough light where she could see him striding to the back of the boat, something silver clutched in his hand.

A gun? What was he doing with a gun?

Lord, no!

Driven by a need to prevent his demise, Lizzie ran toward him, hoping she wasn't too late. When she reached the platform, she screamed, "Don't do it!" to his back.

"Sorry, but I have to," he muttered, and without turning around, he aimed the gun and unloaded bullets into the water several times.

Lizzie stood stunned, wondering what in the heck he had killed. Some unsuspecting fish? Dinner? Gosh, she was hungry. No time to consider that now.

He fisted his free hand at his side and clutched the

gun in his other. "I'll be a son of a.... Damn it straight to…" He blew out an angry breath.

It was perhaps the most skilled censorship she'd ever witnessed from a man. A nice thing, Lizzie decided. She didn't want Baby Hank exposed to too much foul language.

After walking to Jack's side, she saw nothing but a carousel of bubbles floating on the water's surface. "What did you murder?"

"Your basket. The thing wouldn't go away."

She braced her hands on her hips and stared at him with ire. "Was it really bothering anything? I mean, that poor defenseless gondola has witnessed marriage engagements, golden anniversary celebrations, played host to Boy Scouts. Now you've sent it to dark, watery depths to become fish food."

"The fish won't touch it."

"Then explain to me what harm it was doing, hanging on to your boat?"

He crouched with the gun gripped in his hand between his parted knees and his eyes focused on the sea. "Probably no real harm."

"See there—"

"Until I shot it."

Now she was really confused. "I don't understand."

He rose and tucked the gun into the back waistband of his jeans. "I heard something scrape. I think I just sheared off the damn prop."

Served him right. "It wasn't working anyway. And don't you have a spare?"

Wrong thing to say, Lizzie realized when his

steely gaze snapped to hers. Had it not been for the baby, she might have dived overboard and tried to make it to shore on her own.

"This isn't Oz," he said in a low, tempered voice. "No magic here. This is serious business, Dorothy."

Dorothy? Wasn't he just the funny man tonight. Two could play that pet-name game. "And it called for killing the gondola, *Ahab*?"

"I did what I had to do."

Lizzie knew what she wanted to do—sock him. But she deplored violence, and guns, so she settled for a direct verbal assault. "Well, I wish I would've brought my little dog, Toto. I would've sent him into attack mode. For protection, of course."

His frown deepened. "You don't need protection from me, I assure you." He held up his gun. "I've never had to use this before, but it's necessary when you're out to sea alone. Unfortunately, I just wasted all my bullets."

She laid a dramatic hand across her forehead. "For a minute there I thought you might put your poor disabled boat out of its misery, or use it on yourself in a moment of desperation."

"You thought wrong." He angled toward her and studied her long and hard. "What you did a minute ago, chasing after me knowing I was armed, wasn't a very smart thing to do. For all you knew, I could've meant to harm you."

"You could've done that by not saving me earlier, but you rescued me anyway. So I figured you wouldn't murder me, even if you did massacre Bessie."

"Bessie?"

"My balloon. And that wasn't too smart, either."

"It's an inanimate object, Dorothy."

"An inanimate object with propane tanks, Ahab. You could've blown us back to Kansas."

He hinted at a smile, but it didn't form all the way. "You're right. I wasn't thinking."

"And I wasn't exactly thinking when I rushed at you knowing you had the gun. I only knew I didn't want you to hurt yourself."

He took a step closer. "Why?"

A weird question. "Because everyone deserves to live, even if they are a bit cranky."

He took one more step. "Cranky?"

She couldn't exactly back up without being obvious, and for some reason she didn't really want to. "Yeah. Cranky. Not that you don't have a reason to be a bit put out." She studied her bare feet, unable to look at him directly, not with him so close that she could count the whiskers on his chin and the character lines around his assessing eyes. "I'm sorry. Really I am. I do appreciate everything you've done for me and Hank."

"Hank?"

She raised her gaze to his and smiled. "My baby."

He looked as though she'd announced she intended to birth a skunk. "You call your baby Hank? For God's sake, why?"

"My father's name was Hank. He died almost two years ago. I've never known a stronger, kinder man."

Lizzie saw a glimpse of guilt in Jack's eyes before

his gaze dropped to her belly. "Then you know it's a boy?"

"No. I only confirmed the pregnancy this morning, so it's too soon to tell." And what a way to celebrate the news, stranded with a sullen sailor. "But I hope it's a boy. Not that I don't like girls. I've just always gotten along better with men."

His features mellowed, from staid to a tad less stoic. "That's good to know considering I'm a man, and you're a woman, and we're going to be spending a lot of time together. In very close quarters."

Had that really sounded like a sexy, sinful guarantee? *No way,* Lizzie thought. *No how. Not her and him.* "Then we're really—"

"Stuck. Together." A slight smile surfaced. "You and me, babe. Until someone happens to come along."

First princess, now babe. He had a lot to learn about her dislikes, and she was more than willing to teach him. "I am not a babe, and doesn't anyone know where you are?"

Any inkling of a smile disappeared from his face. "I haven't talked to anyone for a year, except for a few people in port, and now you."

A year? Had he been without a woman for a year? The prospect that her virtue might be in peril momentarily crossed Lizzie's mind, and yes, somewhat excited her, but he really didn't seem to be in an amorous mood. Except for his proximity. Except for his eyes. He kept looking at her in a way that made her flesh threaten to crawl up her neck and over her head, pleasantly so. In fact, just thinking about him making love to her doused her whole body in slow, scrumptious heat. How goofy to even consider that. Obviously she had been visited by the hormone fairies.

Lizzie snapped her thoughts back on the situation at hand. "I'm sure Walker will send someone out to look for me."

Finally, he put some distance between them. Now Lizzie could breathe normally instead of pant.

"Who is Walker? Your car?"

"Ha, ha. The head of the chase crew."

He looked hopeful. "And he saw you drifting?"

"As far as I know, he did. When I came awake, I tried to contact him but I couldn't pick anything up on my radio. That leads me to believe I drifted farther off course than I'd realized."

"You have a radio?"

"I did. It's kind of submersed at the moment."

"Then I guess we'll have to rely on your good fortune."

"Or yours."

He looked altogether too serious, and almost sorrowful. "Apparently my good fortune ran out a while ago."

Lizzie didn't dare ask what life-altering event had driven him onto his boat, by himself, for months, away from all humanity. She'd already done enough damage for one day; no need to rock the boat, figuratively speaking. "Okay. I'm fairly lucky most of the time."

"Good, because the last time I checked the

weather, there was a storm heading our way. That's the reason I was returning to port.''

"Until I fell from the sky.''

Finally, he smiled all the way, stripping years off his handsome face. "Yeah, but them's the breaks. Just as long as you know what you're up against. The weather could get pretty rough.''

Living for years in Ohio, smack-dab in the middle of tornado alley, Lizzie had grown up with storms. She had overcome her fear and learned to respect their majesty, their power. Come to think of it, not much seemed to frighten her because long ago she'd learned you just have to have faith that things would work out.

However, Jack Dunlap did frighten her in a way, or maybe it was his sensual pull. Not that she would tell him that. She didn't dare reveal her attraction to him. In fact, she was determined not to let him see that each time she was close to him, she entertained some really dubious thoughts.

Lizzie pulled her gaze away from his lest she give herself away. "I'm sure everything will work out fine.''

"Just so you know," he added, "it might get rocky around here." His eyes narrowed and he took on *that* look again. The one that said he meant business, she'd like to think the kind that involved undressing and caressing. "Can you handle it?''

Oh, yeah. "Oh, sure. What's a little wind and rain?'' A little bedtime adventure.

Halt, Lizzie.

"In the meantime," he said, moving a bit closer,

"I'll have to show you what I need you to do in case the situation calls for it."

Visions of him instructing her on the finer points of lovemaking leaped into her brain. What a way to weather a storm. She could consider that later. First, she needed food.

Her stomach rumbled loud enough to rouse the Loch Ness monster. "Maybe this is a really bad time to ask, but do you have anything to eat? I'm starving."

His grin went wicked and a little wild. "So am I, Dorothy. So am I."

Jack was very hungry, thanks to the woman busily raiding his cabinets. He should've thought twice, ten times before he walked in on her in the tub. He should've turned around and headed out the door. He should leave her to her own devices now, before he did something really ridiculous, like run his hands down her bare thighs, then up again, then down again....

He had to get his libido in a choke hold and put it to rest. Not necessarily an easy prospect, and only a momentary remedy. He had no idea how long this little liaison would last, or how he would control himself as he spent time with a woman who possessed a strong will, sassy mouth and a body that would be worth investigating. A really nice mouth that he'd wanted to kiss into silence several times today. Right now, even. But she was pregnant with another man's child, and he didn't want that hassle, no matter how tempting she could be. He had more than enough to worry about considering his disabled boat.

"Don't you have anything besides canned meat?" she asked, slamming one cabinet door closed and moving on to the refrigerator.

"I like canned meat. It's convenient, and it's not half-bad once you get used to it."

After closing the refrigerator door, she leaned back against it. "No salad?"

"Not at the moment."

She threaded her bottom lip between her teeth. "This is not a good thing. I'm a vegetarian for the most part, although I will have poultry on occasion."

"Maybe you should consider diving for seaweed."

She rolled her eyes to the ceiling. "You are so amusing, Ahab."

"Say what you will, but there's nothing better than a big juicy rare steak."

"Rare?"

"Yeah, the rarer the better."

Lizzie's hand suddenly went to her belly, her face as pale as the white galley counter. "Oh, gosh. I think I'm going to be sick."

Jack rushed to her side and guided her up the companionway. She removed her hand from her mouth long enough to ask, "Where are we going?"

"To the deck," he said. "I have a rule. Anyone who gets seasick has to do it over the side."

"It's probably morning sickness," she muttered, her words muffled by her palm.

But it happened to be night, Jack thought. He

guessed a little nausea was possible. After all, what did he know about pregnant women? Not a thing. He had a feeling he was about to learn more than he'd ever imagined.

When they reached the stern, he turned her toward the sea and held on to her from behind. "Go ahead."

She glared over one shoulder. "I can't do it with you watching."

"You're going to have to because I'm not letting you go. If you fall in, then I'll have to go get you. And babe, I'm thinking that would be a bad idea. Rule one, stay on the boat."

That brought her around in his arms. "I told you, I'm not a babe."

"And I'm not Ahab."

"It's either that or Captain Hook since we seem to be following a fairy-tale theme."

"Both my hands are intact." Definitely so because they'd somehow made their way to her hips.

"I guess you're right about that, so Ahab it is."

He couldn't hold back his smile. "Okay, Dorothy. Are you feeling better now, or do you still need to be sick?"

She drew in a deep breath, thrusting her breasts forward against his chest. Man, he didn't need that.

"I'm not nauseated anymore, only hungry," she said. "I just need something to eat."

Jack needed to kiss her, badly. But he sure couldn't do that at the moment, or anytime for that matter. He took a much-needed step back but kept his hands clasped loosely around her waist should she decide to pass out. "Look, I have some Oriental noodles with vegetables. Will that do?"

She grinned. "Perfectly."

How little it seemed to take to please her. Jack wondered if that held true in all endeavors, including lovemaking. Slapping the thoughts from his brain, he released her completely. "Let's get you something to eat."

"And Hank," she added.

Even though it was the last thing he wanted to do, Jack laughed. For the first time in months.

The man kept staring at her. Oh, he'd tried not to be too obvious about it, but four times now Lizzie had caught Jack watching her mouth.

Egad! She probably had a Chinese noodle hanging off her chin. Her fingertips immediately zipped to the area, but thankfully she found no strings. Just in case, she grabbed a napkin and swiped at her mouth to remove any latent residue.

He glanced up from his bowl again and this time his eyes homed in on her breasts. Lizzie immediately looked down at her chest, expecting to find a nice brown blob smeared on the borrowed T-shirt. She always seemed to miss her mouth, very odd since it was a more than adequate size.

Nope, no blob. Just cotton. Fairly transparent cotton that didn't come close to hiding the fact she was still a bit chilled.

Sheesh. Is that what he'd noticed? Well, if so, she'd just have to cover the evidence.

Sitting back in the chair, Lizzie folded her arms

across her breasts. "That hit the spot. Not exactly my favorite, but I feel much better now."

"Good," he muttered, dropping his gaze to his food.

"I'm really not that opposed to meat unless it's beef. I love cows. My grandfather named his herd after the grandchildren. Then one day I learned we were having my cousin, Bernie, for Sunday dinner. Literally. Well, not literally. The cow named Bernie. That was the end of that. No more beef for me."

Jack murmured something Lizzie couldn't quite discern. Obviously he wasn't too willing to join in the conversation. She wouldn't let that stop her. "There are lots of replacements for beef, though. Take ground turkey, for instance. Have you had any?"

He glanced up for a moment then resumed pushing the last of his disgusting stew around in his bowl. "Not in a while."

"Oh, so you have had some?"

"Of course."

"Then I assume you'd agree that it's not so different from having a regular hamburger."

His gaze snapped up. "Huh?"

"You know, a big juicy hamburger with all the fixings. Yum, yum."

He frowned. "That's a weird comparison."

"Why? When considering ground turkey versus ground beef, I'd say it was an accurate comparison."

"Turkey? You were asking me about turkey?"

"Yes, what did you think I was...?" Reality dawned through Lizzie's own confusion. This was so rich. "Wait a minute, you thought I was asking you if you've had any…." She couldn't finish her sentence, or contain her laughter.

Jack didn't laugh nor did he look at all amused. "I obviously misunderstood you."

"Obviously. Did you really think I would ask you about your sex life?"

"My mistake."

She leaned forward and propped a cheek on her palm. "Well, do you have one?"

He looked away but not before she saw discomfort in his eyes. "I don't want to go there."

Oh, but Lizzie wanted to. She wanted to know more about him since they would be sharing their time for a while, and whatever else they might decide to share. She was suddenly very warm. "I imagine a man like you has certain needs to fulfill. And I imagine there are plenty of women at your beck and call to take care of those needs. You know, a woman in every port."

After pushing his bowl to one side, he clasped his hands in front of him and stared at her. "Think what you will, but I don't care to discuss my love life."

"Then you do have a love life."

"Not anything to write home about." He looked as if he'd regretted making that admission. Lizzie was glad he had. At least now she didn't feel so alone in her celibacy.

"I can relate," she said. "My love life is more or less nonexistent."

That recaptured his attention. "Obviously you had one at some point since you're pregnant."

If he only knew the real circumstances behind the pregnancy. One couldn't be wined and dined by a plastic catheter. "You're right, let's not go there."

His crooked smile made a sudden showing. "Ah, come on now, Dorothy. You started this."

She stood. "And it is now finished, Ahab."

The lights flickered as Lizzie carried their plates to the sink. She stopped and stared at the ceiling. "What was that?"

Turning, she found Jack with his head lowered, the bridge of his nose pinched between two fingers as if he had one heck of a headache. Then came a long, frustrated sigh. "The batteries are going down. It's only a matter of time before the lights go out completely."

"Then we're going to be completely in the dark?"

He looked up. "Yeah."

"Do you have any candles?"

"Another rule. No candles on the boat, which means we need to conserve power."

So much for creating a romantic ambience, Lizzie thought. "Flashlights?"

"A couple. But I'm out of extra batteries. I do have a kerosene lantern we can use until that fuel runs out."

Just peachy. Lizzie leaned back against the counter. "Does this mean we're going to have to eat cold food?"

"Yeah."

"And take cold showers in the dark until we're rescued?"

"Yeah. But I was planning on that anyway."

Coming to his feet, he headed toward the stairs. "Until the water runs out."

"Where are you going?" Lizzie asked, following behind him in case he decided to shoot something else.

"To light some flares."

"Can I help?"

He stopped and faced her. "You can watch."

"That's no fun," she said with a grin. "I'd really rather participate."

He inclined his head. "Would you?"

"Yes. Don't you think it's more productive when two people get in on the act?"

"That depends on the act."

In a fit of feminine insanity, she brushed her bangs away from her forehead and attempted a coy look. "Did you have a particular act in mind?"

His silver eyes darkened with something mysterious and promising and overtly sensual. "Flares, Dorothy. We're going to ignite some flares."

Something else was igniting. Something new and different within Lizzie. Something combustible that had to do with chemistry, and not the kind one studied in high school. Combustion between a man and woman. Between Ahab and Dorothy.

Maybe Captain Jack didn't want to acknowledge it now, but he would if Lizzie had any say-so in the matter. They were stranded and had to find some way to pass the time. Life was short, and no one could predict the future. She might as well go for it because this chance might never come again. The chance to experience what it would be like to have a strong, brooding sailor make love to her. A live, virile man. For the very first time.

Then once she returned to her life, she could take the experience with her. And on those lonely nights, she would bring out the memories to keep her company.

If Jackson Dunlap could be persuaded to cooperate.

Three

Jack sent up the flares, only two tonight. He'd save the other two for later if these didn't happen to summon assistance.

"Oh, wow."

He glanced at Lizzie who watched the cloudy sky with wonder, as if the display of light had been provided for entertainment.

"They're so pretty," she said, turning her amazing smile on him. "I remember thinking that very thing while watching *Titanic*."

Good, God. "I don't think we should go there, either, Dorothy."

"Oh, pooh. It was a nice romantic movie, if you overlooked the ship sinking."

"That's my point. I'd rather not discuss sinking ships."

"I guess you're right." As she backed up to the railing, her smile vanished but it didn't detract from her wholesome looks. With her wispy layered blond hair framing her face, her wide, guileless blue-green eyes, she seemed almost childlike at times. Yet her body shouted woman. Jack's gaze automatically drifted to her full breasts outlined against the thin fabric, confirming that fact.

Dragging his attention back to her face, Jack tried desperately to ignore her current state of undress, but with her wearing only his shirt and, he suspected, nothing else, his attempts at detachment were futile.

She didn't seem to notice though, much to Jack's relief. "Do you think someone will find us?" she asked evenly, but she couldn't mask the concern in her voice.

"Eventually."

She seemed doubly disturbed despite the reappearance of her smile. "Maybe in a day or two, right?"

He couldn't bear to shatter her optimism, or to cause her more anxiety. "Probably." *If* someone happened upon them. *If* the Coast Guard had been notified of their disappearance. *If* the storm didn't hinder any kind of rescue. And if they were lucky, they had twenty-four hours left before they had to deal with that.

Determined to provide some hope, he said, "Look, we still have plenty to eat. Of course, you might have to give up your dietary requirements for the time being."

Her hand came to rest with reverence on her abdomen. "I will do that for Hank's sake. He needs food." She wrinkled her nose. "Even if it is some kind of questionable goulash."

Jack admired her commitment to her child. Admired her ability to look on the sunny side of the situation. If only he could be that sanguine, but unfortunately he was far too jaded in general, in spite of his financial success.

The waves picked up, jarring the boat. Lizzie lost her footing and luckily Jack was close enough to catch her, close enough to smell her feminine scent mixed with sea air as she looped her arms around his neck.

"Whoa there, Dorothy."

"Sorry. Guess I don't have my sea legs yet."

She had great legs, Jack thought, and they were brushing against his at the moment. Even though he was wearing chinos, he could still imagine how her bare skin would feel against his. How she would feel beneath him.

He really should let her go, but what if she fell again? She did, closer against him. "Isn't good balance required when you're in a balloon?" he asked, surprised at the grainy quality of his voice, at his body's swift reaction to her nearness. At his resistance to turn her loose, which had absolutely nothing to do with courtesy.

"Not really," she said in a wistful tone. "You have very little sense of movement in a hot air balloon. It's as if you're standing still, and the whole world is falling away from beneath you."

Jack experienced that same sensation at the moment. He felt as if something inside him was falling away, namely his opposition to anything that threatened his solitary life, his emotional fortitude. "Sounds great."

"It is great," she said on a sigh, her eyes linked with his as solidly as her arms circled his neck. "It's incredible."

So was she, Jack decided. Incredible attitude. Incredible eyes, both wise and innocent. Incredible breasts pressed against his chest. And a very incredible mouth. Although it made no sense, he wanted to know that mouth intimately. Soon. Now.

There was no wisdom in his contemplation, no hesitation in the kiss. He simply took it, grabbed for the brass ring, as he'd done most of his life. Success had not come to him without risk, but the way Lizzie responded to his exploration—the slide of his tongue against hers, the way phenomenal heat coursed through his body—this attraction to her was more than risky.

As if he'd literally been burned, Jack pulled her arms from around his neck and placed her hands on the rail to steady her. Unfortunately, he wasn't feeling all that grounded, and it wasn't due to his lack of sea legs. "I don't know why I did that."

She touched her lips with long slender fingertips. "I know why."

"Yeah? Mind explaining it to me?"

Her grin came with the force of a gale. "You're a boy, and I'm a girl. It's nighttime, and we just enjoyed some fireworks."

He couldn't deny that. He also couldn't deny that

he wanted her in a big way, but he couldn't act on that need. He had to remember she was pregnant and needed much more than he could give, emotionally speaking. He had to remember that in a matter of days she would be gone, and he would be back to his old life, exactly the way he wanted it—alone, with no concerns beyond his own welfare. With no worries of letting anyone down.

"Sorry," he said. "It won't happen again."

With one hand braced on the railing, Lizzie slipped the other down her side, over her hip, and back up to her waist where she planted it, as if displaying her wares. And some nice wares they were. "You're sounding mighty sure of yourself, Ahab."

At least he'd sounded that way. "I am. Now let's go. It's time for bed."

"Is it really now?"

He balanced on releasing a very descriptive oath. "Yeah. You can sleep in my bunk, and I'll take the fold-down sofa."

"Isn't your bunk big enough for both of us?" she asked in a raspy, seductive voice.

Not in this lifetime. "I'd probably roll on top of you."

"What a horrible prospect."

Did the woman know no shame? Did she know what she was doing to him with every innuendo she uttered? Damn straight she knew. For some bizarre reason, she'd decided to play with him, in every sense of the word. And as bad as he wanted to play, Jack wouldn't. He couldn't.

A woman like Lizzie needed stability, not a man

who had spent his adulthood recklessly searching for adventure at every turn. She needed something solid and secure, a man who wouldn't fail her.

His first priority—his *only* priority—was to keep her safe until they again reached shore. Even if he was having a helluva hard time avoiding the fantasy of making love to her.

Lizzie had never been one to put much stock in fantasies, at least where men were concerned. Yet every night since the day she'd tried to get pregnant, she had fantasized about her baby's father. She knew only what the fertility clinic had volunteered—German heritage, mid-twenties, just over six—feet tall, brown hair, hazel eyes, a recent college graduate who happened to be very smart. Magna cum laude, in fact. She really liked that part. Not that she hadn't been proud of her accomplishments. Just because she'd chosen the creative route instead of academics didn't mean she couldn't hold her own in the intelligence department. After all, she had been top in her cosmetology class. The best darned aesthetician in the whole school, as a matter of fact. She had a gift for transforming women into what they envisioned themselves to be, at least from a superficial standpoint.

Unfortunately, she'd never been able to physically transform herself, not that she'd really wanted to. She had no use for makeup. Who needed the hassle of flaking mascara and reapplying lipstick on an hourly basis? Maybe she wasn't anything special in the looks department, but she knew who she was and what she wanted from life. She had scrimped and saved, squirreled away her tips in order to try her hand at the balloon business. With the demise of Bessie, it looked as though it might be a while before she could start over again.

No problem. She would still have her little one. She only hoped that her child would inherit her creativity and his father's brains. A nice balance.

Lying back on the pillow in Jack's "bunk"— which happened to be queen-size—she allowed the steady rock of the boat to lull her into bliss, but it did nothing to bring about sleep. Oh, well. She would just try to imagine the man who had fathered her child.

She saw only Jack Dunlap.

If only she could get him out of her mind. But how could she? The man was sleeping in the next cabin wearing who knew what. Maybe nothing. That consideration brought about both chills and steam running helter-skelter through her body.

How silly she'd been to think that she could actually seduce him. They certainly hadn't taught her that technique in school. How ridiculous to believe that he would fall into her bed with the bat of an eyelash. If she chose to consider she couldn't even entice a man who'd obviously been by himself for months, then she would definitely be depressed. So she just wouldn't think about it at all.

But she couldn't quit thinking about *him*, his handsome features, his sober demeanor, his occasional smile that could knock the floor out from under her if she hadn't had good sense to ground her. Not to mention his strong arms earlier on the deck. Boy, had he smelled great. He'd felt great, too. And come to think of it, he'd kissed even better.

Though he hadn't taken her up on her offer for a little night magic, he had shown some signs of life when, for reasons unbeknownst to her, he had decided to give her mouth a try. Maybe he'd been trying to shut her up.

Rolling to her side, Lizzie curled up into a ball and attempted to generate some heat. Thoughts of the good captain's lips aided her somewhat, but she could still use some extra covers. Might not hurt to tell Ahab good-night since an hour ago he'd pointed her in the general direction of the bedroom then left her alone. She didn't like being alone.

On that thought, she slipped out of bed and padded into the adjacent living area. The room was shrouded in darkness, the boat continued to sway and she accidentally knocked her knee on the sofa's arm.

She stifled her urge to yell out in pain for fear that she would startle Jack, and he might have found more bullets.

"Are you awake?" she whispered.

No answer.

"Ahab?" she called, this time a bit louder.

Still no answer.

Having somewhat adjusted to the limited light, she moved toward the sofa now made into a bed and used her hands to feel for Jack, a rather pleasant prospect. He wasn't there.

Most likely he was in the bathroom, she decided, and cautiously made her way in that direction. When she didn't find him there, she realized there were only two possibilities—he was up on deck, or he'd abandoned ship.

Lizzie really didn't think he would leave her alone to fend for herself. Of course, she had been known to drive people crazy, but she'd never driven anyone overboard. She supposed there was a first time for everything.

Opting to alleviate her concerns, she made her way to the deck and released a breath of relief when she found him standing with his back to her at the railing, frozen like a berg as he stared out to sea. The steady stream of clouds in the overcast sky only revealed a partial glimpse of a three-quarter moon in brief intervals. No visible stars whatsoever and the wind was eerily calm.

Yet even in the muted light he looked imposing silhouetted against the fathomless horizon, strong and forbidding. Mysterious and seductive.

With catlike steps she approached him. "Are you okay?"

At the sound of her voice, Jack tensed. He'd been tense since he'd kissed her, every bloody inch of him. And in all honesty, he was anything but okay at the moment, especially now that she'd made another unexpected appearance when he'd thought she was safely tucked into bed, asleep. His bed.

Turning, he thanked his unlucky stars that he couldn't make out much more than her form. He didn't need to get another good look at the ultrathin, short shirt that revealed too much leg and the outline of her breasts. But it really didn't matter considering all that he imagined underneath her limited attire.

He cleared away the images and the hitch from his throat. "I thought I'd keep watch for a while, just in case someone saw the flares."

She took a step forward. "No luck, I take it."

"No, no luck. But it's fairly foggy tonight." The current conditions complemented his hazy mind.

"Maybe someone will come soon." She hugged her arms tightly around her and moved closer.

The railing behind him kept Jack from backing up. He didn't really want to back away, but it might be best before he did something incredibly insane, like kiss her again, or lay her down on the deck without formality.

"Can't sleep?" he asked, knowing in fact that he couldn't if his boat's survival depended on it.

"I'm trying, but I'm a little cold. I thought maybe you might have an extra blanket I could use."

He almost offered to keep her warm. Almost. "Yeah. In the armoire next to the bed. Top shelf."

She hesitated a moment, the sudden silence as thick as the night mist. "Are you coming in soon?"

"In a bit."

"How long is a bit?"

Surely she wasn't going to proposition him again. If she did, he might be tempted to take her up on her offer despite the fact he shouldn't. "I don't know. A few more minutes, I guess. Why?"

She turned her face to one side, allowing Jack the benefit of her pleasing profile. "If I tell you why I want you inside, promise not to laugh?"

He wanted to do a lot of things. Laughing was not one of them. "I'll try to restrain myself." Solid advice he should heed where she was concerned.

"You're going to think I'm a big chicken."

Considering she'd displayed little fear after her ordeal, and she'd chosen to raise a child on her own, he could honestly say he'd never known a more courageous woman. "I seriously doubt that."

"Yes, you will." .

"Try me." If only he could allow that in the literal sense.

She sighed. "I really don't like being alone."

Funny, Jack thought, since he preferred to be alone. "You don't live alone?"

"No…yes. I didn't until last week. My roommate, Ian, moved in with someone else."

"You had a male roommate?"

"A very good friend."

"Only a friend?" Now, why had he asked that? And worse, he'd actually sounded jealous.

"Yes. You seem surprised."

He was. Very. "Personally, I'd have a hard time living with a woman for an extended period and keeping it on a platonic level."

"You don't have any women friends?" Now she sounded shocked.

"No, guess not."

"You really should try it." He saw a flash of white teeth and heard the smile in her voice. "Maybe it would enable you to get in touch with your feminine side."

He'd rather get in touch with her feminine side.
"So were you and this Ian pretty close?"

"Yes, you could say that. Until he found the love
of his life."

From her tone, Jack wondered if she hadn't been
completely honest. Maybe she'd had a thing for this
guy at one time. It was none of his business, but he
had to ask. "Is he the father of your child?"

"Oh, no. It wasn't that way between us. I worked
with him at a day spa and salon, before I established
my balloon business."

"Is he gay?"

She scowled. "Not every guy who cuts hair for a
living is gay."

"I didn't mean that. I meant it seems kind of odd
that you and he wouldn't have…you know. Gotten
together."

She glanced away. "It wouldn't have worked. Ian
has always been very fond of beautiful women. His
newest girlfriend is a model. So you can see why I
wouldn't be his type."

Jack pondered that for a moment. Obviously she
had little insight into her attractiveness, a basic
beauty that went far beyond physical qualities, not
that she was lacking in those either. Maybe she didn't
see herself as model material, but Jack sure as heck
had noticed all her finer points, and she had more
than a few.

She was also full of surprises. Considering her iron
will, he would never have guessed that she'd have a
problem with being alone. Quite different from his
attitude. "I've personally found that it's not so bad

being by yourself. Fewer problems that way. No having to get used to another person's habits.''

''Ian was the perfect roommate,'' Lizzie said adamantly. ''He was always there when I needed him.''

''But not anymore, huh?''

''Oh, he'll always be there, just not in the same way. I'll try to find a new roommate when I get home. Or I might wait until after the baby's born.''

''Another guy?''

''Probably. But until then, I'll manage just fine.''

''Then what's the problem tonight?''

She shrugged. ''I guess it's because this is a strange place. Strange sounds and stuff. I'll feel more comfortable knowing you're in the next room.''

He'd only feel more comfortable with her in the next country, and his discomfort had centered itself below his belt. Right now it was all he could do not to touch her, kiss away her concern, make love to her until dawn. Maybe even after dawn.

Why the hell he wanted to do all those things, Jack couldn't say. He barely knew her. He had yet to spend twenty-four hours with her. And she was pregnant. But he had to admit that the moment he'd laid eyes on her, he'd wanted her in some crazy, elemental way.

Lust, pure and simple, he tried to tell himself, even though he couldn't recall the last time a woman had affected him so strongly. Admittedly he had desired a few women after only limited contact, but that had never gone beyond animal attraction.

Lizzie was different. Lizzie was special. Lizzie

was driving him to distraction and she probably would as long as she graced his boat.

"You are cold," he said when he noticed her slight tremor.

"Yeah, it's a bit chilly out here, especially when you don't have on a whole lot of clothes."

He didn't need to hear that, or think about it, but he did. In vivid detail. His sail suddenly went to full mast, and not the one on his boat. Even though she probably couldn't see his current predicament, Jack turned his back to her. "I'll be down in a few minutes. I promise."

"Okay. I'll be fine until then. Just stick your head in the door and let me know that you're back."

He'd like to do more than that. He'd like to climb into bed with her and warm her up with his hands and his mouth. "I'll be sure to do that." If only he could do more. He could, but he wouldn't.

Gripping the rail, Jack let out the breath he'd been holding when he heard the sound of footfalls heading away from him.

"One more thing, Captain."

So much for a return to normal respiration and slow deflation. "Yeah."

"You have a really nice boat."

"Thanks."

"And your butt's not so bad, either."

"Ahab, what is this?" Lizzie called from the head the next morning.

No way was Jack going to make the same mistake

again by walking in on her during her bath. "What is what?"

"This big silver bowl behind the bathroom door. It looks like some kind of a trophy."

It was, the last he'd won before tragedy struck. The last good race. "I use it as a doorstop." Not exactly the truth. He didn't want the reminders so he'd hidden it away when the memories had become too overwhelming. He'd basically forgotten it was there, intentionally so.

The bathroom door creaked open and Jack braced himself for Lizzie's appearance. Hopefully she'd put her own clothes back on.

All hope faded when she appeared before the sofa where he was now seated having his coffee and a strong urge to kiss her again. She wore his yellow polo that stopped at her thighs, but unlike the T-shirt it had a slit up each side, allowing him a glimpse of the curve of one buttock and, fortunately, her underwear. At least she had those on, not that it really mattered. She could be wearing a trench coat covering flannel pajamas and it wouldn't make a difference to Jack and his persistent parts.

She presented him with her usual smile. "Hope you don't mind but I rummaged around in your drawers last night."

Jack would have definitely remembered that. "What drawers?"

"Your bathroom drawers, looking for a spare toothbrush. I found one and used it. Hope that's okay."

He only minded that she was way too cute to ignore. "That's fine."

She removed the towel wrapped like a turban around her head, bent forward and began furiously drying her blond hair. "You'd be so proud of me. I barely used any water. Just enough for a good spit and shine."

At the moment she was giving Jack quite a show, her bare breasts visible because of the open collar on the shirt. He tried to look away but his eyes might as well have been cemented to her chest. The more she rubbed, the more she jiggled, and the more she jiggled, the more Jack squirmed.

Finally, she straightened and surveyed his face. "Is something wrong?"

Yeah. He was hard as a handlebar with no relief in sight. "I didn't get much sleep." Thanks to her.

"You know what you need?"

Oh, yeah. He knew exactly what he needed—to take off what little clothes she now wore and get down to business. "No. What do I need?"

"A haircut. And a shave wouldn't hurt."

"I've already shaved. Early this morning."

"A heavy beard, I see." She narrowed her eyes and studied him as if she was an artist sizing up her subject. "If you have a pair of scissors, I could cut your hair."

"I'm not sure I trust you to do that."

"You should. I was a stylist before I opened my balloon business. I'm rather good."

He would just bet she was. "Maybe I like my hair the way it is."

Seating herself on the sofa facing him in a display of long limbs and feminine wiles, she brought her bent knees to her chest. "Just a trim so it will be a little neater."

Man, she was stubborn. "If I let you do this, will you leave me alone to work on the boat?"

"Sure. I'd like to work on my tan."

"Last time I checked, there wasn't any sun."

"Are you sure?" She scooted off the sofa, walked to the porthole and drew back the curtain. "That looks like the sun to me."

When Jack finally took his attention away from Lizzie's legs and brought it to the window, he realized she was right. He would've wagered his fortune that the skies would remain overcast. Maybe he shouldn't be at all surprised. If Lizzie wanted sun, she would probably get sun. In fact, he figured she was rarely denied anything if she put her mind to it.

"You better hurry and get out on deck," he said. "I doubt the sun will be with us for very long."

She turned from the window. "First, the haircut."

No point arguing with her, Jack decided. "Fine. The scissors are in the galley, third drawer to the left of the sink."

"I'll go get them and you take a seat at the table." She tossed him the towel. "Slip off your shirt and wrap this around your shoulders."

He saluted. "Anything else, Major?"

She laughed. "You're the second person who's called me Major, but I believe the last time it was followed by 'pain in the butt.'"

He rose from the sofa and slipped his shirt over

his head then tossed it aside. "Are you always so high maintenance, Dorothy?"

"Not really, Ahab. I'm just the kind of person who knows what she wants and then does her darnedest to get it."

Not so unlike him, Jack thought. He'd spent his life being that driven.

Right now Lizzie looked as though she wanted something from him, something sweet and seductive, apparent by the way her gaze slid over his bare chest.

Her eyes widened and so did her smile. "You're in really great shape. Do you work out often?"

He had one particular workout in mind, but it didn't involve weights. "Only in the sense of maintaining the boat."

She moved closer. "I guess you just come by it naturally, then."

In order to get his thoughts back on course and his body back under control, Jack said, "Speaking of working, I'm going to try and get the engine to turn over. The alternator charges the batteries so we'll have some lights."

Following a sexy shake of her hair, she sauntered toward the adjacent galley. "I really don't mind the darkness, as long as you're here."

Jack wasn't totally in the dark about what she intended to do with him, to him. She'd been doing it since her arrival. Question was, would he have the strength to deny her?

A day ago, he might have said yes. But today, he wasn't at all sure about anything, except for the fact that Lizzie Matheson was totally disrupting his life. And he was beginning to like it.

Four

The man had a fine head of hair to match his equally fine bod, Lizzie thought while she started to work on Jack's trim. She didn't like cutting hair dry but she didn't dare ask him to wet it considering water was a precious commodity. While he sat silently in the swivel chair anchored to the dining-room table, she started with the back, snipping a little here, layering a little there. She had one heck of a time keeping her attention on her task, especially when she moved in front of him and faced his remarkable chest peeking out from the towel she'd draped across his broad shoulders. If she didn't do a better job of concentrating, he'd end up with a reverse Mohawk.

Fine strands of hair rained down onto the towel and she took the opportunity to periodically brush them away, noting that every time she flicked her fingertips over his chest and belly, his muscles tightened. This had to be the most fun she'd ever had giving a man a haircut.

"Are you almost done?" Jack's voice fell somewhere between a growl and a plea, the first words he had spoken since she'd begun.

"Patience, Ahab. You have a lot of hair."

"Until you got your hands on it," he muttered.

She could continue for an hour and still have plenty to work with. "You know something, your boat really needs a name."

He glanced up at her, a hint of irritation in his expression. "It has a name."

She slid her fingers through his hair, enjoying the soft texture against her palm. "So what is it?"

"Hannah."

A woman's name. Lizzie probably shouldn't be surprised at all, nor should she be jealous. But she had to admit she was. Naming a boat after a woman was as intimate as having a woman's name tattooed on a body part. She wondered if, in fact, Jack did sport a tattoo in places she had yet to see. Maybe she should do a full body search. That thoroughly nice thought made her shiver.

"Is Hannah someone special?" Her voice came out sounding like an animated version of her own, high-pitched, nervous.

"Yeah, she was."

Was? It dawned on Lizzie that maybe this Hannah person, whom she already disliked strongly, possibly broke Jack's heart. Maybe that was why he'd taken to the sea, alone. Maybe he was still pining away for the shrew.

All the more reason to take his mind off his troubles, Lizzie decided. Of course, he hadn't been all that cooperative. Somehow, someway, she would concoct a plan, a means to convince him that they might as well make good use of their time together. She doubted anything permanent could ever exist between them so she would settle for temporary. An affair.

She'd never had an affair and perhaps that was why it sounded so harsh, unfeeling. Still, emotions would have to remain absent from the mix. No problem. After all, she prided herself on her sound emotional stability. So what if she cooed over kittens, cried over movies, sighed at love songs? She vowed to remain grounded.

Remaining grounded—literally—became a chore as the boat pitched, swayed, and then pitched again. She fell forward against Jack with her breasts practically adhered to his face.

He nudged her back and stared up at her, his palms planted firmly on her hips, his silver eyes dark and intense. "You're dangerous, Dorothy."

She anchored her hands on his broad shoulders— solid strength curved against her palms. She attempted a weak smile. "I dropped the scissors behind the chair, so I'm not armed."

"Yeah, you are." His gaze homed in on her breasts. "Your body should be registered as a lethal weapon."

Lizzie's body felt like a miniature grenade, ready

to detonate if he so much as touched her intimately. She wished he would touch her. She wished he would give up that steel resolve and pretend for one second that she was a desirable woman.

As if he sensed her longing, he traced a slow line with one long finger down the crevice between her breasts, exposed by the sagging placket on the shirt that was much too big. His eyes followed the movement and so did Lizzie's. With fascination she watched his blunt fingertip move up again, then down again, tracing the chain at her neck before stopping at the middle of her chest where the button created a barrier. With little effort, he freed the button, then another, leaving the fabric gaping, leaving Lizzie winded and wanting as she'd never wanted before. An odd little sound escaped her mouth.

He brought his gaze to her lips and his hand back to her hip, probably to push her away. Lizzie kept her eyes pinned on his, challenging him to continue. She saw a glimmer of hesitation before he parted the fabric wider then lowered his head to streak his tongue down the path his finger had taken.

Oh my, oh my, oh my... Oh, yes.

"You're too damn tempting," he murmured against her chest.

The next thing Lizzie knew, she was being swept up into Jack's strong arms. He fell back onto the couch, bringing her across his lap. The towel had fallen away from his shoulders during the move and Lizzie took advantage of the moment while Jack took her mouth with a breath-robbing kiss. He wrapped one arm around her shoulders, holding her close against him while his right hand gently kneaded her breasts beneath the opening of the gaping shirt. She sent her own hand on a journey across the mat of hair on his chest, her fingertips playing his nipple much the same as he played hers. His tongue made passes between her lips almost in sync with the sway of the boat.

Jack dropped his hand from her breast and much to Lizzie's delight, slipped it beneath the shirt's hem. Never before had she wanted a man so badly, wanted him to soothe the intimate ache, which seemed exactly where Jack was heading as he palmed her abdomen. Then as if her belly had grown fangs, he pulled his hand back.

He broke the kiss and looked at her for a long, torturous moment. "We can't do this."

As easily as he'd scooped her into his arms, he slid from beneath her and stood, leaving her sprawled out on the sofa, the shirt gaping and her legs parted in a very unladylike manner.

"Where are you going?" she asked, her voice laced with frustration and unanswered need.

He snapped up his shirt from the sofa's arm and slipped it back on. "I'm going to try to start the boat."

Obviously he was bent on leaving her in a state of sexual suspension. Anger took the place of unanswered desire. "You're a tease, Ahab."

He scowled. "I'm smart, Dorothy. You and I both know this is stupid. You're pregnant."

She scooted up on the sofa and planted her feet on the floor. "I'm not deceased." She leveled a pointed look at his distended fly. "And neither are you."

"I don't intend to get tangled up with anyone."

"Is that emotionally or physically?" she answered with defiance in her tone.

"Neither."

Lizzie came to her feet and stared at him straight on. "Why is that, Ahab? Did someone break that heart of yours?"

He streaked a hand over his shadowed jaw. "No, Dorothy, no one broke my heart." He said it with conviction, leading Lizzie to believe she'd been on the wrong track where his past was concerned.

She took a determined step toward him. "Then why did you bail out from life? What drove you here, all alone on your boat?"

"I like being alone. I don't want any complications."

"I didn't ask you for forever, did I? It's only a means to pass the time, Ahab. A man and a woman taking pleasure in each other. Nothing more complicated than that." Something that was totally alien to Lizzie, and probably the reason why the declaration sounded phony, even to her own ears.

He sent her a suspicious look. "That's all you want is sex? I don't believe it."

"You don't know anything about me."

"I know that I'm not the man you need."

"I never said I needed a man, at least not in the way you're suggesting."

His ensuing smile was cynical. "Maybe not, but

you're the kind of woman who can make a man forget who he is, what he wants.''

She moved before him and touched his cheek. ''What do you want, Jack Dunlap?''

''My solitude.''

With that he turned and made his way toward the bow, leaving Lizzie alone to deal with her disappointment. But she had to admit he was probably right; he wasn't the man she needed. In fact, she had never needed a man other than her father. She hadn't needed a man to have a baby, at least not all of one. Then why did she have this almost desperate need for Jack Dunlap? Because she had basic feminine needs? If so, Lizzie had no clue why he'd been the one to arouse those desires.

But it was more than that. She'd always been a sucker for lost souls, and Jack Dunlap was as lost as any man she'd ever known. Oh, he had tried to hide it beneath an iron facade, but Lizzie had witnessed a glimpse of vulnerability, of pain, in his eyes.

Needing a diversion, Lizzie opted to continue with her plan to enjoy the sunshine while it lasted, even if her attitude had taken a sour turn. She strode into the bathroom, yanked an oversize towel from the cabinet then rummaged around for some sunscreen. Not finding any, she decided she would have to limit her time outside. Besides, Jack had already generated enough heat within her; she didn't need to go totally up in flames.

Lizzie stomped onto the bow and shook out the towel with a vengeance then laid it on the fiberglass deck, muttering an inventory of insults aimed at her very stubborn host. She paused for a moment to consider her clothing situation. She had no swimsuit, only a bra and panties. Her bra was still hanging in the bathroom. She could go retrieve it, or she could go topless. Who would see her anyway? The captain of the ship, but only if he decided to seek her out, and she doubted he would. Even if he did, he'd already seen just about everything.

Lizzie stretched out on her belly wearing only her panties, her cheek resting on her folded arms. The sun beat down on her back as her heart beat a crazy rhythm in her chest when she recalled their interlude. Jack had wanted her—that much she knew—a least from a physical standpoint. He'd said she was tempting. Apparently not tempting enough to entice him into a little extracurricular activity. Chances were, he'd probably had plenty of women in his bed. Women who were more experienced, more sophisticated, more beautiful.

Lizzie wasn't really any of those things, nor had that bothered her before. She'd been happy just being herself, and she still was. If Jack didn't appreciate her qualities, too bad. After they were safely back on land, she would leave him behind to start over, make plans, make a good life with her child.

Who could ask for more?

Lizzie could. Oh yes, she could. She couldn't deny that having a real father for her baby—a wonderful father like her own—was nagging at her. She couldn't deny that having the love and respect of a good man was, too. Even though it was silly to consider that Jack might be that man, she refused to give up on him even if he'd given up on himself. If she couldn't gain his complete attention, then perhaps she could learn more about him, learn what made him so sad, aid in bringing him back to the land of the living. It was definitely worth a try.

If Jack could harness the energy below his belt to power the boat, they could return to port in record time. Several times he'd glanced out the windows of the interior pilothouse at Lizzie who was lying half-naked within his view, to his libido's detriment. She had no idea he was watching her, didn't have a clue what she was doing to him at that moment. She was driving him nuts with her questions, driving him to distraction with her sensuality. Worse, she was threatening to make him let down his guard.

Five more seconds on the sofa and he would have known every inch of Lizzie's knockout body. If he hadn't had the presence of mind to remember she was pregnant, right now he would probably have his hands all over her and his mind on anything but their predicament.

The sensual visions kicked his body back to life and caused him to release a harsh groan. He didn't need this. He didn't need her. Hell, he didn't need anything except a return to his normal life. He did need to make sure that she was safe while in his care. But only safe, and that didn't include sex.

Regardless, he couldn't seem to stop imagining what it would be like to make love to her. Would all that passion for living she retained manifest itself during lovemaking? Probably, and a very dangerous prospect. He'd been serious when he'd told her that he didn't want any complications. Lizzie could be one giant complication. She already was. Not only did he want her, he liked her. He liked her smile, her wit, her easy manner. And man, she had eyes that could stop him dead in his tracks. Eyes that damn well seemed to see through him. Everything he should avoid in a woman. But he couldn't avoid her.

He also couldn't keep focused on anything but the vision she presented outside the tinted window as she lay stretched out before him—the curve of her back, the dip of her spine, the rise of her buttocks highlighted in great detail by the sun's rays. At least she was on her stomach, keeping her fantastic breasts from view.

She raised her head for a moment and stared up at the sky. Then she abruptly stood, snatched up the towel and sprinted off the deck. Jack wondered if she'd noticed the bank of clouds moving toward them and maybe feared being struck by lightning. If anyone deserved that fate, it would be him, considering his questionable thoughts.

"Ahab!" echoed from down below followed by a flurry of footsteps.

Jack moved from the helm and stood at the top of the three steps leading to the pilothouse. "Up here."

Lizzie appeared at the bottom of the landing and stared up at him, the towel wrapped around her and excitement flashing in her blue-green eyes. "I saw a plane flying above us!"

The best news he'd had in days. "Coast Guard?"

She frowned. "No. I think it was a private plane.

I didn't stay on the deck long enough to make out too many details.''

"Did you try to flag it down?"

"Of course not. Are you insane?"

He was getting there. "That would be the logical thing to do."

She pushed her hair back from her face. "I was practically naked. I didn't want anyone to think I'm some sort of exhibitionist."

"Fine time to get modest on me, Dorothy," he muttered.

"Well…I mean…the pilot could have been an older gentleman. I wouldn't want to be responsible for giving him a heart attack."

Jack was balanced on having a little cardiac flare-up himself with her standing there wearing only a towel—a towel that hit her midthigh. One quick flick where she'd knotted it between her chest and it would drop to the ground at her feet like an anchor.

She looked contrite. "I'm sorry, Jack. I wasn't thinking."

"That's okay. They probably would've thought you were just being friendly." He brought his attention back to the view outside the window. "I'm guessing the storm will be on us soon."

Lizzie stood on tiptoe and stared in the same direction. "It still looks fairly far in the distance."

"Yeah, for now."

He noted the alarm in her eyes when her gaze snapped to his. "Surely someone will rescue us soon."

If only he believed that. "Hopefully. In the meantime, I need to secure everything. We probably have a few hours, tops. The storm will probably hit at some point this evening, if not before.''

"I guess we'll just have to ride it out, huh?''

Damn her sunny attitude. Damn the images of taking her on another kind of wild ride. "Yeah.''

She flashed another beaming smile—then flashed him. Parted the towel and gave him a good glimpse of her bare breasts. "The offer still stands if you'd like a nice way to pass the time.''

The offer wasn't the only thing still standing. "Dorothy, one of these days your offers are going to get you into trouble.''

She tucked the towel back into place. "Gee, that's the kind of trouble that could be mighty fun.''

She swiveled on her heels and swayed back toward the main salon. Long after she was gone, all Jack saw was Lizzie Matheson. Him and her. Tangled together.

The boat's motor might fail to start, but Jack's motor was running full force.

Lizzie washed off with a damp rag and put her clothes back on, all of those she'd had on her person when she'd arrived on Jack's boat. Obviously she could dance stark naked on deck and Jack wasn't willing to give an inch—in both a literal and figurative sense.

When she left the bathroom, she heard the sound of voices. More than one. Had they been rescued?

Lizzie sprinted up the steps to the deck to find Jack speaking to two men pulled alongside the boat in a smaller craft. One guy sported a scruffy goatee and a dirty white cap; the other man had a severe flattop and looked as if he hadn't missed a meal a day in his life.

Jack had his back to Lizzie, so she couldn't see his reaction to their visitors. She suspected he was greatly relieved. If they could catch a ride back to port, then he would be rid of her, once and for all.

When Lizzie made her way to Jack's side, Scruffy winked at her. "Howdy, ma'am. The captain here didn't tell us he had a pretty lady on board."

Oh, get real. Lizzie decided he'd been a charm-school reject. "We're certainly glad to see you guys. For a while we thought—"

"That we're the only fools out here," Jack interrupted.

"Having some problems?" Flattop said, leering at Lizzie as though she were an all-you-can-gorge buffet.

"The engine's not working," Lizzie responded.

Jack sent her a cautioning look. "We're having a few problems. The mainsail blew out and my engine's having problems cranking. I'm working on that now."

"We can give you a ride back to port," Scruffy offered.

Lizzie grinned. "That would be—"

"Unnecessary." Jack slipped his arm around her waist, taking Lizzie by surprise. "We don't want to leave the boat. My wife and I are on our honeymoon."

Wife? Honeymoon? Lizzie bit back the urge to say

she was still impatiently waiting for the consummation.

Jack brushed a kiss across her lips, shocking her into silence. "We haven't really minded being stranded, if you catch my drift."

The seedy duo cackled. "Yeah, we know exactly what you mean," Scruffy said, followed by another wink. "Anything we can do? We wouldn't mind taking your lady back to port with us until help arrives."

Jack gave Lizzie another squeeze. "I can't stand being a moment without her."

Flattop pulled a toothpick from his shirt pocket and flipped it between his bulbous lips. "Well, we'd be glad to call for help but our radio's shorted out. Problems with yours?"

"Yeah." Jack sounded as if he didn't want to make that admission. "I should have it repaired soon."

Scruffy shot a glance over his shoulder. "Hope you get it fixed soon. The storm's looking real bad, a nasty northwesterly that's gonna push you out to sea. That's why we're going in. Hate to have to cut short our fishing trip because of the weather, but that's just luck of the draw."

Lizzie tried to temper Jack's scowl by turning on the sugar-sweet act. "Do you fellows mind notifying the Coast Guard when you're back in port?" She whisked a kiss over Jack's jaw and patted his chest. "My *husband* and I would greatly appreciate it."

Flattop started the boat. "Will do. In the meantime, batten down the hatches. It's gonna get rough.

The weather service is calling for gale-force winds. Are you sure you don't want to ride back with us?''

"She's sure," Jack said gruffly.

Lizzie felt the first tiny frisson of anxiety over the loss of their only human lifeline, and she used the term "human" loosely. "Thanks, but I'll stay here with my hubby. He'll take good care of me."

Jack tensed against her side as Flattop said, "Good luck and have a good time." Their raucous laughter could be heard over the engine's roar as they sped off.

Once they disappeared over the horizon, Jack dropped his arm from around Lizzie and started away.

"Wait a minute, Ahab."

He turned, his expression taut, his eyes holding the cast of concern. "What?"

"Why didn't you let me go with them?"

He folded his arms across his chest, looking altogether perturbed. "Not a banner idea."

"Why? If I'd gone with them, I could have made the call for help myself."

"You would have never made it to port. Those guys would have had their way with you then tossed you overboard."

"How do you know that? They looked pretty harmless. I mean, they're fishermen."

"Did you see any fishing equipment?"

Lizzie thought a moment. "No, I guess I didn't, but then I wasn't paying that much attention."

"Well, I was, Dorothy. Chances are they're smugglers."

"Maybe you're wrong. Maybe they're what they say they are, just innocent fishermen."

"Innocent?" Jack's laugh held no mirth. "Didn't you notice the way they looked at you? You have no idea what men like that could do to a defenseless woman."

"I'm not entirely defenseless, Ahab. I'm not stupid, either."

"You are too trusting, Dorothy. Your sassy mouth might work on me, but it wouldn't help you with those two miscreants."

"My sassy mouth works on you?" She sauntered up to him. "How does it work on you?"

His gaze slipped to the mouth in question. "It drives me crazy."

She laced her hands around his neck and pressed against him. "Is that in a good way?"

"Lizzie, behave yourself."

She wiggled against him. "Why?"

"Because I'm not going to kiss you again, dammit."

This time Lizzie opted to let it go—for now. She dropped her arms and took a step back. "So what now, Ahab?"

He glanced away. "We wait and hope they do call someone. If not, we'll just have to ride out the storm the best we can."

Not the answer she'd wanted. "Jack, be honest with me. Just how bad is our situation?"

He let go a harsh sigh. "The batteries should be down completely by dusk. The water's just about gone. We have enough bottled water and food to last a couple more days. Unfortunately, we're drifting away from shore, right into the storm's path.''

Lizzie refused to believe that someone wouldn't come to rescue them soon. She refused to believe that Jack couldn't find some way to keep her and Hank safe, get them back to shore, if not tomorrow, then the next day. She refused to believe that they wouldn't survive the storm. If she didn't, she would give in to fear, and she refused to do that, too.

Her hand automatically went to the necklace at her throat. Hadn't her dad always told her that her mother was her guardian angel? And now he was with her, both of them watching over Lizzie.

Lizzie sent up a quick prayer to her mom and dad, the same as she had when she'd spotted Jack's boat the day before. Her parents hadn't failed her then; they wouldn't fail her now.

Feeling a bit more relaxed, Lizzie presented Jack with her best smile, albeit a shaky one. ''I know it will all work out, Ahab. I feel it in my bones.''

His smile came halfway but it didn't conceal the concern in his eyes. ''I'm going to trust you on that one, Dorothy.''

Lizzie laid her palm on his jaw. ''I trust you, Jack. I know that you'll do whatever you can to keep me and Hank safe.''

Jack watched Lizzie return below, burdened by the faith she had bestowed upon him. She had no idea how cruel and unpredictable the elements could be, how even the most skilled sailor could easily become the sea's victim. She had no clue that he had once thought himself capable of mastering the rankest of storms. How quickly he had learned that arrogance was no match for nature. How in one horrendous moment he had suffered the loss of two of his most faithful friends because of a choice he'd had to make between saving his crew and a woman who never should have been onboard in the first place. His weakness to resist that persistent woman had cost him. It was still costing him, at least when it came to his peace.

And now he was charged with keeping another woman safe, a woman who was carrying a child. But Lizzie was there due to unforeseen circumstances, not because she'd insisted on being there. Lizzie didn't have a selfish bone in her incredible body. She'd disregarded his shortcomings, never looked upon him with judgment. She believed in him. She deserved to be safe, and he intended to keep her that way if at all possible.

The thought of failing her ate at him like salt on ice. He had to believe that fate wouldn't be so cruel as to let that failure visit him again.

Five

Jack sat across from Lizzie at the dining-room table where they had recently finished a cold canned-meat dinner. Green-gray ominous-looking clouds had gobbled up the sun an hour before and the faint rumble of thunder could be heard in the distance. Although the sea was currently smooth as glass, Jack realized that it only signified the proverbial calm before the storm.

Lizzie shoved her plate aside and frowned. "I really hate this."

He sat back in the chair and surveyed Lizzie's face cast in the golden glow of lantern light. He saw only a hint of worry there, but it was enough to fuel his own. "Sorry, Dorothy, but this is the best I can do. That's all the food we have and the batteries are completely drained."

"It's not the food or the dark. I hate this waiting, the not knowing when the storm is going to get here." She leaned forward and took on the familiar hopeful expression. "Do you think maybe it's missed us?"

Jack wished it had, and he considered telling her it was possible. He wished he could assure her that their suspect visitors had called for help, but he had grave doubts about that. And even if they had, there were no assurances anyone would begin a search for two people who obviously weren't in immediate distress except for the impending storm, another factor that could hinder a rescue attempt. Besides, he'd given the miscreants the impression that they didn't really care to be rescued. And if Lizzie's balloon had drifted to shore, her friends had probably given up hope that she was still alive.

No, he didn't want to cover that territory tonight, or worry her more. But Lizzie deserved some honesty. At least he could give her that much. "The barometer's been dropping for the past hour, so it's probably only a matter of time before the storm hits."

"I know all about barometers. A storm is the worst thing that can happen during a balloon flight." She drummed her fingers on the table and looked around, then her gaze came back to rest on him. "You're really worried, aren't you?"

"I've weathered storms before." He didn't dare tell her about the one that had gotten the best of him.

"Is there something we should be doing?" she asked.

"I've secured everything down here as best I can. All we can do now is wait and see what happens." And hope.

She snapped her fingers. "I know one way we could pass the time."

"Not that again," he murmured.

She propped her elbows on the table and rested her cheeks on her palms. "Actually, I was wondering if you have a deck of cards."

"Yeah. Why?"

"We could play a few games of poker to distract us."

As Jack watched Lizzie slide the gold chain dangling from her neck back and forth, another kind of distraction jumped into his brain and it had nothing to do with a friendly game of cards. "I suppose we could play a few games." Anything to keep his hands occupied.

She slapped her palms on the table. "Great. What are we going to use for bets?"

He picked up the blue-and-red box of matches. "We could use these."

"Not very challenging, but I guess that will have to do." She grinned. "Unless you want to play strip poker."

That was the last thing he needed to consider at the moment. "I can probably find some spare change."

She sighed. "Matches are fine. I'll clear the table, you get the cards. We could probably use a couple of flashlights, too."

Jack could use a whole lot of strength, something

that became more than apparent after he followed Lizzie into the galley kitchen and reached around her to retrieve the cards from a drawer where Lizzie was tossing the paper plates into the trash bin. When she straightened, he brushed against her bottom, inadvertently, he'd like to believe, but he knew better. His personal barometer went on an upward climb. Time suspended in the close confines as he stood behind her, pressed against the curve of her buttocks much closer than he should. If he didn't escape soon, he'd end up forgetting himself and his vow to concentrate on what was most important—safety, not sexual satisfaction.

He took a step back and after they returned to the table, he handed her a flashlight and doled out what few matches were left in the box.

Lizzie shuffled the cards like a Vegas dealer and when she was done, placed the deck on the table. "So what's it going to be?"

A long, hard night, Jack decided. "Your call."

She raised a thin eyebrow. "Exactly how good are you?"

"At cards?" If she hadn't known the path his thoughts were taking, she certainly did now.

She smiled. "Yeah, at cards."

He tried to affect nonchalance in light of the pressure building beneath his briefs. "I can hold my own."

Her laughter filled the cabin, a burst of buoyant exhilaration. "I am not even going to touch that."

"That's too bad." Jack mentally chastised himself

for the innuendo, but it had vaulted out of his mouth before he could stop it.

She inclined her head, a hint of wicked mischief reflecting from her blue-green eyes. "Maybe we should play seven-card *stud* in your honor."

"You have high expectations, Dorothy."

"I have good instincts, Ahab."

He leaned forward, his hand resting within touching distance of hers. He really wanted to touch her, badly, and not just her hands. But he knew where it would lead, and why he needed to prevent that from happening. "Maybe we should keep this simple." Sound advice in all regards.

She laid the flashlight on the table to provide more light. "Okay. Five-card draw. You cut, I'll deal."

Jack decided he should leave and cut his losses before he did something really stupid, like clear the table and take her right there without consideration of the storm or the circumstances. She was going to have a baby, and he was going to have one helluva time remembering that fact.

Suppressing a groan, he cut the deck in three piles. Lizzie picked up the cards and began to deal, her sandy eyebrows drawn down in concentration. Once she was finished, she nailed him with a seductive look that made his pulse pick up a notch. "Just so you know, I'm not very good. At cards, that is."

Jack shifted in his seat. "Just follow my lead."

"Oh, I intend to."

As suspected, Jack soon discovered that Lizzie was lucky and much more skilled than she'd claimed.

She won four hands to his one and before long, he found himself down to his last bet.

He turned his cards faceup and pushed them toward her. "I fold. Looks like the game's over."

She stuck out her lip in a pretty pout. "Come on, Jack. The least I can do is give you a chance to win back your losses."

"I only have one match left."

"I could loan you a few." She shuffled the cards again. "But I tell you what. If you lose this time, then I'll find some way to collect."

He could only imagine what that entailed. "And how do you plan on doing that?"

"Why don't you just take a chance and see?"

He was already taking a huge chance, sitting here with Lizzie Matheson, wanting her more than any woman he could think of in recent history. He was torn between his responsibility to protect her and his desire to make love to her regardless of the dire situation they could soon find themselves in. "That sounds dangerous, Dorothy."

"I assure you I won't make you do anything you don't want to do."

Good sense told him to refuse. His libido didn't care to listen. "If you insist."

"I definitely insist."

Lizzie dealt him another hand that could only be termed as sorry as mud soap. The best he had was a pair of twos. Lizzie had a royal flush, both in her hand and on her face.

He met her gaze and saw a flicker of something

that looked a lot like I-want-you. "Guess I lose again," he said.

Slowly she rose and moved around the table to stand before him. "Maybe we both win."

When she swiveled his chair from beneath the table, Jack thought it best to issue a protest. "Lizzie, I don't think—"

"I only want a kiss as payment, Jack. Now would that be such an awful prospect?"

He didn't find anything awful about it, and that was the problem. "Only a kiss?"

She rested her hands on his shoulders. "Sure. Kissing is very underrated, you know." She bent and brushed her warm lips across his forehead. "A very nice reward, in my humble opinion." She placed another kiss on his cheek. "I, for one, enjoy kissing a lot."

And so did Jack, he realized, when her soft lips pressed against his. She slipped past his resistance with a sweep of her tongue, slipped into his mouth, forcing away any thoughts of protest. While Jack gripped the sides of the chair to keep from pulling her into his lap, Lizzie put everything into the kiss, meeting his tongue in a series of gentle thrusts that reminded him of another kind of thrust. But it only lasted a moment before she backed away and returned to her chair.

Lizzie tugged at her T-shirt and cleared her throat. "Now where were we?"

On a fast track to trouble, Jack thought. "I believe I've repaid you so let's call it even."

"Not yet," she said, running her fingertip across

one discarded card, feeding the fire in Jack's gut. "I kind of like this game."

So did Jack. Too much. "What happens if I lose this time?"

"I don't know. I'll have to think on that one."

After Lizzie dealt the next hand, Jack ended up with three kings and two aces. Unable to resist Lizzie's lure, he turned his cards facedown and said, "Bad hand again, and I'm out." Out of his mind. Out of his element considering his voluntary loss of control.

She stood, approached him again and held out her hand to him, palm up. "Give it here."

Confused, Jack asked, "Give what here?"

"Your shirt."

"I thought we were going to avoid strip poker."

"I never said that and you owe me. I'm collecting."

Jack came to his feet, deciding it was futile to ignore Lizzie with the mouth made for sin and the body to match. He crossed his arms, pulled his shirt over his head and handed it to her. "Happy now?"

She took a long visual excursion over his bare chest then her gaze came to rest on his fly. "Looks like the little captain is very happy."

"Little?"

She rested a dramatic hand across her chest. "I'm sorry. Poor choice of words. Jackson Junior then. J.J. for short, figuratively speaking. I certainly wouldn't want to insult your manhood."

His *manhood* was anything but insulted. And leave it to Lizzie to name it. "No offense taken."

When her hand headed toward his chest, Jack caught her wrist. "Lizzie, if you so much as touch me, I can't be responsible for what I might do."

"I'm not asking you to be responsible for anything. I'm a big girl. I'm responsible for my own actions. And right now I really want to touch you."

"I don't think you understand what you're doing to me."

"Oh, I think I do." She wrested from his grip without difficulty, probably because he wasn't trying that hard to stop her.

Jack stood stock-still when she breezed her palms across his chest, released a ragged breath when she tested his nipples with fine fingertips, exhaled slowly when she slid her hand down to his stomach clenched tight against the onslaught.

Again he stopped her by clasping her wrists. "We don't need to be doing this."

The look she gave him was laden with frustration. "Maybe I need it, Jack. Maybe I need to forget about what we might be facing. Have you considered that?"

He had only considered that she was melting his resolve, little by little. He hadn't thought about the fact that she did have needs that he was quite capable of tending, even if he didn't plan to tend his own.

With a forearm he cleared away the table. Matches and flashlights and cards flew in all directions like hailstones battering a sidewalk. When he came to the lantern, he was a little more careful placing it on the deck.

Lizzie's lips parted in surprise when he lifted her

onto the edge of the table and tugged her shirt over her head, tossing it onto the floor atop the debris. He parted her thighs and moved between them, knowing he had totally lost his will. Knowing that in a matter of moments he was going to do what he'd promised himself not to do.

He paused to study her delicate shoulders, the rise and fall of her breasts. He drew a path with one fingertip down the chain and lifted the dual medallions hanging at the end. "Special keepsakes?"

"Good-luck charms."

He dropped the medallions in favor of tracing the outline of her bra. "Do they bring you luck?"

"That remains to be seen."

Without any more thought of the consequences, without any more contemplation of the impending storm, Jack trailed kisses down her jaw and lingered at the pulse point below her right ear, then trailed a damp path to the cleft of her breasts.

He wanted more than a look, more than a touch. He wanted to know how she would sound when he tasted her. But first things first.

Reaching behind her, he snapped the bra open, worked his fingertips beneath the straps at her shoulders and slowly pulled it down her arms, hesitating before he removed it completely. "Are you sure this is what you want, Lizzie?"

"Yes, it's what I want."

Jack didn't see one whit of protest in Lizzie's eyes, only a flicker of desire. Not that Jack expected her to stop him. She had made it quite clear from the beginning that this was what she wanted, although he didn't understand why. Analyzing her reasons was the last thing he wanted once he pulled the bra completely away and tossed it aside.

He'd seen her naked on more than one occasion but this was the first time he'd taken the opportunity to really look at her even though the limited light cast shadows on the details. Her breasts were high, round and beautiful, accented by pale tawny nipples. He would almost be satisfied just looking at them. Almost.

Jack wondered if her heart pounded as hard as his did at that moment, if she had a clue how much he wanted to touch her, to be inside her.

No longer satisfied with simply looking, he bent his head and settled his lips on one nipple. He was mildly cognizant of her hands threading through his hair, molding his scalp, pulling him closer, encouraging him to draw her deeply into his mouth. He was also vaguely aware that the wind whined at the windows and the boat's sway had picked up speed. But the roar in Jack's ears, the carnal haze filtering into his mind, drowned out everything but the soft sounds Lizzie was making and the feel of her against his tongue.

After paying both breasts equal attention, he slid his mouth back up the column of her throat and moved on to her lips. She opened to him and suckled his tongue as he had suckled her, driving him to the brink of madness. In a reckless rush, he pulled her hips forward and brought her to him where he could experience her bare breasts against his chest and the dampness where his mouth had been. He needed this closeness, needed to know more of her. And he knew she needed more from him, very evident when she locked her legs around the back of his thighs and clung tightly to his neck as her pelvis tilted upward against his groin.

He worked his hand between them and unsnapped her pants then tracked her zipper down. Not enough room, he realized when he could barely work his fingertips into the opening.

Somewhere in the logical recesses of his mind, he knew it would be better for Lizzie if he took her to his bed. But in his bed he wouldn't be able to leave it at this. He intended only to satisfy her, give her what she needed despite the fact his own need was producing a mind-blowing ache that screamed to be satisfied.

Leaving her mouth, he worked her pants and panties down her legs, allowing them to slide to the deck, leaving her completely open to him. He watched her face as he slipped his fingers through the light shading between her thighs, finding her warm and wet and ready, finding her center with the pad of his thumb while he pushed one finger inside her.

She released a ragged breath and a soft whimper that he muffled with another kiss. He fondled her with slow, deliberate strokes timed with the gentle thrust of his tongue. He loved the way she felt, loved the way she responded as she lifted her hips against his hand, urging him forward.

When he felt her body quake, only then did he break the kiss to watch her. She lowered her head and closed her eyes until he lifted her chin with his free hand and said, "Look at me, Lizzie."

Opening her eyes, she stared at him with a glazed look and a sense of wonder. Her bottom lip trembled and her breath came out in soft bursts of air.

She looked so damn beautiful at that moment and Jack realized how much he had missed this intimacy, not only over the past few months but also in a lifetime of relationships that meant very little in the grand scheme of things. Now here he was, touching a woman he had known for such a brief time, a woman who had thoroughly turned his world upside down in a matter of days.

"Jack," Lizzie whispered, her voice wary as if she feared what was happening.

He brushed a kiss across her lips. "It's okay, Lizzie. This is what you need."

Lizzie was caught between wanting to let go and never wanting it to be over. Jack's tender strokes stripped her of lucid thought, robbed her of her self-control. She relished each sensation, marveled that Jack was so skillfully sending her somewhere she had never been before with only a few measured touches in all the right places.

Her breath caught painfully in her chest when the climax came calling in strong, steady pulses, and re-leased as the ebb and flow of fulfillment slowly sub-sided. Feeling boneless, she dropped her forehead against Jack's broad chest as she absorbed each pulse of pleasure.

But no matter how wonderful she felt, it simply wasn't enough. She wanted more. She wanted to know how it would feel to be thoroughly possessed by a man when she was so vulnerable and open. But not just any man. She wanted Jack, wanted to know his body. Every wonderful inch.

When she reached for his fly, he growled, "Not now. Not here."

Here and now was exactly what she wanted. Maybe at one time she'd imagined losing her virginity in a bed covered with rose petals, not on a table in a sailboat, but she recognized this might be her last chance to find out what she'd been missing. To find out if Jack Dunlap could do justice to her fantasies though she inherently knew he could. "Yes, Jack. Here and now."

He cuffed her wrists loosely with his large hands but she didn't let that daunt her. She managed to work his fly open, managed to free him and realized she had been totally off the mark with the "little captain" comment. No wonder he had been so offended.

Jack braced his palms on the table on either side of Lizzie's hips while he gave her free rein to explore the territory. She marveled at the way he felt to her inquisitive fingers, the way he looked with his jaw clenched as if he was engaged in the ultimate battle for composure. She could tell with each glide of her hand he was on the verge of losing that battle. And what absolute domination she felt knowing how close he was to tossing away his revered control. What sheer unadulterated joy having him practically putty in her hands—figuratively speaking. In reality he was power in her hands. Undeniable male power.

"I'm warning you, Lizzie." He sounded gruff but not at all menacing.

"I've been sufficiently warned," she replied. "And I want you to show me what you can do with this." She emphasized her words by sliding a fingertip up his generous length.

Something snapped in Jack and that might have worried Lizzie had she not been in such a wanton frame of mind. He shoved his shorts and briefs down his thighs then pulled her hips closer to the edge. Lizzie leaned back and braced on her elbows, closed her eyes and waited as she felt him nudge her legs farther apart, waited for him to finally follow through.

A loud crack forced Lizzie's eyes open, forced Jack away from her. Before she could comprehend what was happening, Jack was already putting his clothes back on.

"Where are you going?" she said to his back as he sprinted up the steps to the deck.

"Put out the lantern and stay here," he called then disappeared from sight.

Lightning lit up the cabin in harsh flashes and Lizzie muttered a mild oath, cursing Mother Nature and her terrible timing.

After sliding off the table, she snatched up her shirt from the floor and quickly pulled it on, sans bra, then tugged on her pants and underwear with considerable difficulty due to the boat's erratic movement.

She turned down the lantern and made her way to the steps leading topside, walking like a derelict on a four-day drinking binge. Not only was she lacking sea legs, she felt as though she had no functioning legs at all. She toyed with her medallions with one hand as she looked up to see if she could glimpse Jack. She couldn't discern anything but the closed door.

If she went up on deck, she had no idea what she would find awaiting her. She also had to consider Hank's safety. But what about Jack?

She couldn't stand the thought of anything happening to him. And as odd as it seemed, she couldn't imagine not having him around, even after they survived this latest crisis.

They would survive—she knew it as surely as she knew her own heart. Maybe she was a fool to believe that once they got off this godforsaken boat, something more might exist between them. Maybe she was a bigger fool to think he might want that, too.

But she didn't have time to take that idea out and play with it at the moment. She had to help Jack. If he didn't return soon, she would seek him out— whether he wanted her or not.

Six

A driving deluge assaulted Jack's face as he fought to raise the storm jib in the gusting gale. Lightning fired the sky in brief intervals; thunder echoed in his ears.

Memories assailed him as severely as the rain pelted his face. Memories of another time, another storm when he'd been fueled by adrenaline, spurred by a competitive edge, driven by danger as he laid abeam—side to the waves—even knowing he could roll over and end up mast down. Back then his goal had been to win another race, to challenge the elements like a fool.

Water slapped at the boat like cruel hands, drawing Jack back into the current predicament. He'd be damned if he would let this squall win.

After he returned aft to steer the boat, he thought

his imagination was on overload when he heard the feminine voice. Then he saw Lizzie hugging the bulkhead before him, protected from the elements by only her shirt and pants, her drenched hair plastered to her face.

His name rose above the scream of the wind as she called to him, again and once again.

"Go back down," he yelled.

She staggered forward. "I want to help."

"You can't! Go back below before you're hurt."

A riotous wave charged the bow, sending a rush of water over the deck and Lizzie forward toward the wheel. He clutched her shirt and came up empty-handed except for the gold chain she wore so closely to her heart. As Lizzie worked her way to his side, he reached for her and the necklace slipped from his grasp.

Lizzie clung to his arm and he turned her around, positioning her between himself and the wheel, framing her with his extended arms as he continued to steer into the waves. He tried to wrap the yellow slicker around her, but to no avail. The wind was too strong.

As Lizzie leaned back against him, Jack experienced an overpowering surge of protectiveness, the urgent need to keep her sheltered.

"My necklace, where did it go?" she shouted over the din.

"It's gone."

She laid a shaky hand against her chest. "Oh, God."

When they got out of this mess, Jack would buy

her another just like it. He would buy her a hundred. But a hundred balloons and a hundred necklaces wouldn't benefit her if she got hurt, or worse.

He bent to her ear and said, "Lizzie, think of you and the baby. You have to go back down below."

She shivered and turned her face up to meet his gaze. "Not without you."

Damn her stubborn streak. "For God's sake, there's nothing you can do."

"Can't you steer the boat from inside?"

Yes, he could, exactly why he'd chosen a boat with an interior helm that provided protection during these very conditions. But he couldn't explain to her why he needed to be outside. Why the guilt that still lived so strongly within him drove him to face the storm's wrath head-on, as if he could somehow finally exorcise all those old demons by facing them again.

Another flash illuminated the sky, illuminated Lizzie's eyes that held a trace of anger, something Jack had never seen before in her gaze. "Dammit, Jack, you don't have anything to prove, at least not to me. So stop being dumb and come back inside."

"I will when I can."

She shoved her hair back from her face and glared at him. "Then I'll go back in, but only for the baby's sake. If you don't come in soon before you die, I might have to kill you."

With that she ducked under his arms and stepped from his side. He released one hand from the wheel and held out his arm for her to take. As she stepped back toward the bulkhead, she slowly slid her grip down until their joined hands provided the only physical connection between them. She gave him a beseeching look then let him go, leaving him alone, leaving him feeling as if she'd taken a fundamental part of his soul with her.

After struggling awhile longer, Jack made a decision. If he continued this useless battle with the forces of nature, he could put himself in further peril. He had no doubt that with her good luck and common sense, Lizzie could probably find a way to survive without him. But he was beginning to wonder about his own survival without her. He didn't care to acknowledge those emotions, didn't care to leave himself vulnerable to her. But he also realized he couldn't stand the thought of leaving her to fend for herself.

For Lizzie, he would concede to the storm's fury and return inside. Return to the woman who was beginning to mean more to him than she should—and that in itself posed a danger of a different kind.

Lizzie didn't bother to change out of her rain-soaked clothes before she curled into a corner of the sofa, clutching a pillow to her chest. She didn't want to be comfortable knowing that Jack was outside braving the weather while she helplessly waited for his return.

The boat jarred and swayed, pitched and moaned in the wicked claws of the storm. She kept her eyes closed and silently prayed, feeling bereft because of the loss of her treasured necklace as well as the loss of Jack's presence. What would she do if she really lost him?

No. She wouldn't invite that possibility into her world. Jack was the consummate sailor. He knew what he was doing. He wouldn't let anything happen to her if he could help it. But could he help it? Even with all his skill, would he be an equal match to the storm? And why was he so bent on playing the tough guy when it didn't have to be that way? She suspected it had very much to do with the reasons why he had taken himself out of life in general, taken to the sea to immerse himself in his coveted solitude.

Lizzie had to believe that he would come to his senses. If not, she had to believe that her angels did exist and that they were watching over Jack now. If she didn't, then she would truly be afraid…and alone.

After a time, the boat seemed to settle to a tempered rocking instead of an unpredictable thrashing. The lightning came infrequently now and the whistle of wind seemed somehow quieter. Or maybe she was only fooling herself into believing the storm was moving on.

When she heard footfalls descending the companionway, Lizzie came to attention. She saw the tall, imposing figure moving in her direction, breathed a sigh of relief when she felt the sofa bend next to her.

Lizzie went to her knees beside Jack and rested her hand on his shoulder. His palm came up to cover her hand and they stayed that way for a time, silent except for the occasional creak of the boat and the steady sound of their breathing, rapid at first then slower and slower as if they were finally giving themselves permission to relax.

"Are you okay?" she whispered.

He eased forward and rested his elbows on his knees and his face in his palms. "It stopped almost as quickly as it arrived, right when I started back inside."

"Then you were coming back in?"

His rough sigh echoed in the darkness. "You were right. I was trying to prove it wouldn't beat me this time."

Now they were getting somewhere. "This time?"

"I've been through worse."

"How bad is worse?"

"I don't want to talk about it."

Lizzie wanted to shout but decided to temper her voice in order to persuade him to come clean. "Is that the reason you came out here all by yourself? Did something happen during another storm?"

"I said—"

"I know what you said, but I have to know, Jack. I have to know what's going on with you."

"Why?"

"Because I'm..." *Falling in love with you.* "Because I can't stand to see anyone so sad and so alone."

"I told you I like being alone."

"Oh, you prefer being alone but I don't think you really like it. You're alone because you're punishing yourself for something. Why are you punishing yourself, Jack?"

"It's past history. Finished."

She blew out a frustrated sigh. "It's not finished. Whatever happened to you, it's still as fresh in your mind as if it happened yesterday." She squeezed his shoulder. "You're welcome to tell me about it. I promise I won't pass judgment because of something that happened a long time ago."

"It happened a year ago."

"*What* happened?"

He sat silent for a long moment as if weighing his words. "I was in a race. An important race, or so I believed at the time. We hit a squall off the coast of Australia. I lost my crew."

"And now you feel guilty because you survived."

"Yeah."

"Wasn't there risk involved, and didn't your crew realize that?"

"My crew depended on me and I failed them, all because of a stupid decision on my part to allow someone to come along that had no business being there."

"Another friend?"

"My fiancée."

Fiancée? Jack, engaged? Or maybe even… "Are you married?"

"No. It never happened. She had about as much adventure as she could stand after that. She ended the engagement and moved on to someone more settled."

Lizzie hadn't been wrong to assume that Jack still suffered from a broken heart, shattered because of loss. She certainly could understand that, after losing her dad, but she would never have bowed out of life.

Her father would have hated that. She would've hated that.

Jack abruptly stood, shrugged out of the slicker, tossed it on the sofa then held out his hand to her. "Come on."

She rose and said, "Where are we going?"

"To get out of these clothes and then to bed."

To bed, with him, exactly what Lizzie had wanted so desperately only a few hours ago. Now she wanted answers. "Jack, we need to talk."

"I don't want to talk anymore, Lizzie. I want you with me, in bed. I don't expect anything else."

At least he wanted that much. "Okay, we can do that. But what about the storm?"

"The worst is over."

Maybe the storm outside, but not the one still brewing in Jack, Lizzie decided. Considering what he'd been through tonight, she opted not to push him, at least not now.

She took his hand and followed him into the state-room bathed in soft-wash light coming from the narrow rectangular windows. Surprisingly the moon had made an appearance in the clearing sky, signifying the storm was truly gone. Lizzie's heart lightened with that knowledge but she still felt weighted by Jack's pain—a pain he didn't want to discuss. No matter. He was with her now and he needed some comfort, even if it meant only holding him.

They peeled away their drenched clothing, one article at a time, and piled them on a chair in the corner. Lizzie hesitated, unsure if she should remove her underwear. But when Jack lowered his briefs and tossed them aside, she did the same with her panties. Now here they were, completely bare and about to climb into bed together. Only to comfort each other, Lizzie reminded herself.

An awkward silence hung over the cabin as they each claimed a place on opposite sides of the bed. Jack tossed the covers back and climbed in first then Lizzie followed suit.

They stayed on their backs staring at the low ceiling, only inches separating them. Lizzie hated not knowing what to do, what to say. Then she felt Jack's discernable shiver.

"Are you cold?" she whispered.

"No. More like afraid."

Jack? Afraid? "Of what?"

"Of touching you."

Obviously he considered her to be sexually insatiable. If he only knew that her recent behavior had been totally foreign to her. She'd just have to prove to him she could be in his arms without expecting more.

She rolled to her side and laid her head and one arm on his chest. The covers bunched between them prevented their bare flesh from touching, but Lizzie could still sense his heat—and his reluctance.

"See there?" Lizzie said. "No harm, no foul, just a simple embrace."

Jack slid an arm underneath her neck and rested his palm on his abdomen. "Nothing about you is simple, Dorothy."

"You're so wrong, Ahab. I'm a simple kind of girl. Not all that demanding most of the time."

"Yeah, I guess you're right."

"I bet you go for anything but simple women."

"Like I said before, I don't want any complications."

Lizzie's heart sank at the same time the boat took a considerable dip. Jack tightened his arm around her.

"No complications tonight, Ahab. Just some sleep, okay?"

"I'm not sure I can sleep."

Lizzie took a chance and kissed his cheek. "Sure you can. Close your eyes and count sheep or bottles of rum or whatever sailors count at night. Or we could count our blessings that we made it through this."

He sighed. "Yeah, but we're farther out to sea and we're still not sure when someone will find us."

Lizzie lifted her head and stared at him. "I don't want to hear that. Someone will find us soon. We'll be back on land before you know it."

She caught a flash of a smile in the diffused light. "If you say so, Dorothy."

"You can take that to the bank, Ahab."

And Lizzie realized that when they did return to civilization, it would all be over, regardless that she didn't truly want it to be. But even if Jack disappeared from her life, she would still have her baby—and an empty space in her heart that she knew only time would close.

Right now she needed to concentrate on closing

her eyes, taking to memory these moments in her strong, silent sailor's arms…in case they never came again.

Sleep continued to evade Jack long after Lizzie's breathing grew calm and steady. She'd barely moved for a long time—until she managed to toss her bare leg over his thigh. He remained as still as a corpse, an apt description since rigor mortis had set into one very sensitive part of his body. It was all he could do not to crawl beneath the covers to kiss those long limbs and slide his mouth upward to find out if she tasted as sweet and warm as she felt against his hip.

But he wouldn't do that. She was pregnant and she needed her rest. She needed much more than he could give her beyond an incredible bout of lovemaking. And he knew it would be incredible between them, just as he knew she would awaken in the morning with the same sunny smile that made his emotional fortress crumble a little more each time he saw it.

He settled for holding her closer knowing that when this was over, they would say their goodbyes. She would return to her life and the promise of her child. He would return to the sea with nothing but his seclusion.

Still, he would never regret having her with him, even for the briefest time. He would never be sorry that she'd landed on his boat and in his life.

He might be sorry that he didn't have more to give her in terms of permanency, that he didn't have the guts to open himself up to the possibilities. But they still had some time together, hopefully not more than a day or two, for Lizzie's sake.

As for him, he would try to be strong, resist her body, resist what she had been so willing to offer.

And that could be the hardest thing he had ever done in his life.

Lizzie woke not knowing how long she had been asleep. She did know that her arms were now empty due to Jack's disappearance from the bed. She raised her head to find him staring out the windows that hit him chest high. The first signs of dawn cast the sky outside in a light pink-and-blue panorama, revealing subtle details of Jack's breathtaking back. Lizzie tracked the line of his strong arms dangling at his sides from broad, well-defined shoulders. But when her gaze reached his elbows, she made a little detour to study the path of his equally strong spine that dipped beneath his trim waist. And below that, a sight that could stop a stock-car race—firm, taut buttocks that looked as if they had been calculated to provide hours of entertainment for a pair of eager, feminine hands. Her hands, to be exact.

The realization that Jack wasn't a stick-around kind of guy did nothing to keep her from wanting him as much as she'd wanted him from the beginning.

But did he still want her? Only one way to find out.

Lizzie climbed across the bed and came up behind him. Feeling audacious, daring and a little bit devilish, she slid her arms around his waist and pressed against him.

"You're up early."

He let go a wry chuckle and braced his palms on either side of the window. "You don't know the half of it."

She slipped her hands lower, down the flat plane of his abdomen—and inadvertently got the full effect of all of *it*. "J.J. seems very awake."

He brought her arms up to his chest, but at least he didn't push her away. "I probably should check on the boat. See if there's any damage."

She rested her lips against his back. "Why don't you come back to bed for a while?"

"I don't feel like sleeping."

"Neither do I."

He tensed but failed to turn around. "If I get back in bed with you, we both know what's going to happen."

"A girl can hope."

"That's all that would be between us after this is over."

"I don't expect anything else, Jack. Promise."

"But I can't promise you anything."

"You could promise to stop thinking about it and just do it. You know you want to, and so do I."

A shudder ran through him and Lizzie suspected he was close to giving in. "But you're pregnant," he said. "I don't want to hurt you."

"You won't." Only a little. "Not if you're careful, and I know you will be."

He turned into her arms and taking her by surprise,

lowered his head and kissed her, a joining of lips and teeth and tongues. He clasped her hips and pulled her flush against him. His unmistakable arousal fueled her own excitement, creating a rush of moist heat between her thighs.

As he backed her to the bed then laid her down, Lizzie didn't dare ask him why the change of heart. She only knew that he was here, kissing her neck, her breasts, preparing to give her what she needed, and apparently what he needed, too.

Maybe that was all it was, just primal need, at least for Jack. She could easily need more from him but she wouldn't fall into that sinkhole. She did need to tell him one very important thing.

When his hand traveled down her hip and curled to the inside of her thigh, Lizzie stopped him by clasping his wrist. "Jack, I have something to say."

He lifted his head and stared at her. "You want me to stop?"

She chewed her bottom lip, searching for a way to say what she had to say without sounding like an imbecile. "No, I don't want you to stop, but you might find this a little odd."

"Try me."

"You remember when you asked me about the father of my child?"

"Yeah, I remember."

"Well, I don't know his name."

"A one-night stand?"

"No, it actually took three times."

He frowned. "I'm not following you, Lizzie."

"It took me three times to get pregnant. And I don't know his name but I do know his number."

"His phone number?"

"His lot number. J–34571. I've never met him, but I know his sperm intimately."

"Are you saying you were—"

"Artificially inseminated. I wanted a baby but I didn't have any prospects. So there you have it, I don't know my baby's father and I never will. That's the way I want it."

Jack's features softened. "To tell you the truth, Lizzie, I'm kind of relieved."

Lizzie grinned. "You are?"

He returned her smile. "Yeah. I was a little worried that you weren't being completely honest with me. I thought you might even have a boyfriend or husband waiting for you back home."

"Nope, no boyfriend or husband. No one but me and Hank."

He rimmed her ear with his tongue. "Good."

She framed his face in her palms and forced him to look at her. "There's one more thing."

"Make it quick."

Quick was good. Quick should be relatively painless. No need to beat around the bush, Lizzie decided.

She closed her eyes, drew in a deep breath and blurted, "I've never made love before."

Seven

She might as well have thrown him overboard.

Never in Jack's wildest imaginings would he have expected Lizzie's revelation. Shock speared him as well as stupid male pride over the prospect of being her first.

But with the realization came some heavy apprehension on Jack's part. Not only was she pregnant, she was inexperienced, and the way he was feeling right now, barely clinging to control, he worried he might hurt her.

Needing some distance, he rolled away from her onto his back and rested an arm over his eyes.

"This doesn't change anything, does it?" Her voice was weak, unsure. Very un-Lizzie-like.

"I don't know. I'm thinking."

"I can handle it, Jack."

But could he?

Jack dropped his arm to his side and looked at her. She'd turned to face him with her jaw propped on her palm, her expression optimistic. He had a bird's-eye view of her breasts, flushed and pretty in the morning light. He couldn't stop his gaze from traveling over the curve of her hip and the golden V at the juncture of her thighs. Despite what he now knew, he still wanted her with every molecule of his body and being.

She bent and planted a kiss on his neck then sent him a smile. "Lighten up, Jack. It's not the end of the world. It's just the end of my virginity."

"And you're pregnant."

She sighed. "I've read a lot of books on pregnancy. If I honestly believed I would hurt the baby, I wouldn't be doing this."

He laid his palm on her bent head as she kissed his chest. "Why me?"

"Why not you?"

He could think of several reasons, the first being he probably didn't deserve the honor. The second— she deserved her first time to be with a man who intended to stick around. And there was the fact that she...

Obviously intended to torture him into submission.

Jack's thoughts shut off when Lizzie kept going with her kisses, straight down to his abdomen, way too close to the immediate matter taking precedence over his concerns.

"That's far enough," he muttered.

Lizzie raised her head and frowned. "Why?"

Because if she continued, her first time would be over in record time. "Take my word for it, it's not a good idea. Now get back up here."

"Promise you won't change your mind about seeing this through?"

"And if I don't?"

She gave him another scorching kiss right below his navel. "Then I guess I'll have to keep J.J. occupied until J.S. changes his mind."

The urge to deny her, to feel her mouth engulfing him, tempted Jack to withhold the promise. But this was about her. This would be for her.

"I promise. Now come here."

She shimmied up his body and practically climbed on top of him. He clasped her neck and brought her mouth to his, kissed her with pent-up, unrestrained passion. She moved against him in a steady tempo, sending him close to the edge.

He rolled her onto her back and rose above her to consider what he wanted to do next. What he *should* do next. He knew exactly what he wanted to do. Take a nice easy journey over her body with his mouth.

As if she'd tuned in to his thoughts like some sexy psychic, she asked, "What are you waiting for?"

Certainly not for her to give him the go-ahead. She'd done that time and again. But would taking certain liberties totally scare her off and out of his bed?

He took one look at her expectant expression and immediately reminded himself that this was Lizzie, the woman who gave no thought to going after him when he was armed. The woman who was totally undaunted when she wanted something badly enough. The woman who'd just revealed an underlying sensual side that was waiting to be tapped—by Jack, if he decided to take that course.

Lizzie would handle anything he dealt her on a sensual level and probably with great finesse. As long as he was very careful.

She tapped her fingers on his shoulder. "I'm ready and willing, Jack. Give it your best shot."

He sat up, shifted to the end of the bed and settled one mile-long leg across his thighs. He raised her foot and studied her toes. Her feet were about as pretty as the rest of her.

She shoved both pillows behind her neck and stared at him. "Are you going to give me a pedicure?"

"No."

"Swab the deck? I see you've already lifted the sail." She sent a pointed look at J.J.

Jack couldn't believe he was starting to grow accustomed to one primary body part having a name. Leave it to Lizzie. "I plan to give you the time of your life."

She wiggled her toes. "I'm intrigued."

This time he grinned. "You're going to be more than that, I assure you."

"Promises, promises."

When he planted a kiss on her instep, she giggled. Jack smiled from the simple joy of it. "Are you ticklish there, Dorothy?"

"Just a little bit, Ahab."

He kissed her calf. She giggled again then tried to

look serious. "I'm sorry," she said. "I guess I'm more sensitive than I thought."

Jack smiled to himself when he thought about kissing one sensitive area on her person.

She drew in a deep breath and let it out slowly. "Okay. Continue."

He kissed her knee lightly. She shoved one pillow over her face but it did nothing to stifle the sound of her uncontrollable giggles.

"Lizzie, you're giving me a complex."

"I seriously doubt that," she said, her words muffled by the pillow.

When he whisked his lips above her knee, her chortles turned into full-fledged laughs. Normally that might halt Jack's plan but it only served to make him more determined. He parted her legs and stretched out between them, then kissed his way up the inside of her thigh.

She dropped the pillow from her face.

She wasn't laughing.

"Oh, so you're not ticklish here?" he asked, brushing his knuckles back and forth over the path his lips had taken.

"Uh, no." Her voice was barely a whisper.

Jack felt somewhat pleased that he'd found a way to shut her up, at least to make her stop laughing. But he didn't want her totally quiet once he really got down to business.

On that thought, he slid his tongue up the inside of her thigh but he didn't linger for long. He continued to the slick folds to find the spot that would elicit a moan. Lizzie clutched his head in a death grip while he suckled her until she squirmed beneath his mouth. He slipped a finger inside her, then two, imagining in vivid detail what it would feel like to experience all that heat surrounding him.

He looked up to find her eyes wide with surprise, hazy with desire. Her breasts rose and fell with each labored breath as he continued to manipulate her with his mouth, showing her no mercy. He felt her tense around his fingers, heard her softly moan, but that didn't stop him until every last spasm of her climax subsided.

Jack moved over her, his body raging with the need to take her now. Instead, he smoothed her hair away from her face and kissed her softly. "Are you ready now?"

She closed her eyes. "I think I am."

Jack was concerned over her tentative tone. He skimmed his palms down her arms to discover her hands balled into tight fists. "Relax, Lizzie."

She rolled her neck on her shoulders and shook out her hands like a runner preparing for a relay. "Okay."

This wasn't going to work, not with her wound tight enough to break. On one level Jack could relate. He was wound pretty damn tight himself.

Moving back to her side, Jack breezed his fingertips over one breast, then the other before sliding his hand between her thighs where his mouth had been only a few moments before.

Her eyes snapped open. "Jack, you really don't have to—"

"I want to," he said as he stroked her lightly,

tenderly, insistently. When he detected she was on
the brink of another release, he took his hand away,
parted her legs with his thigh and moved atop her.
He eased inside her a fraction and saw a hint of apprehension in her expression.

Jack's body demanded a hard thrust but his head
told him to take it slowly. He swept his lips over her
flushed cheek. "Are you okay?"

Lizzie nodded and traced her fingertip along his
clenched jaw. "I'm fine. Are you okay?"

"Yeah."

"You look stressed."

It wasn't stress that had him gritting his teeth. It
was sheer sensation, the overwhelming need to be
completely inside her.

"I've never done this before," spilled out of his
mouth before he realized how inane that sounded.

Lizzie looked totally taken aback. "You're a vir-
gin?"

This time he laughed but it held no mirth. "I've
never done this before without some kind of protection."

"Never?"

"Never. I want you to know that I'm safe. I don't
have any—"

She silenced him by pressing a fingertip to his lips.
"I trust you."

He withdrew slightly then slid back inside her a
little more. "You're way too trusting, Lizzie."

Tension showed in her features. "I know that you
wouldn't put me in any danger that way. I know you

wouldn't intentionally hurt me." She winced when he pushed deeper.

Jack froze. "I'm hurting you."

"No pain, no gain, as they say."

"Hell, Lizzie, I don't want to hurt you at all." He slid his hand between them and fondled her above where they were joined. "I want to make you feel good." As good as he felt. As frantic as he felt.

She opened again to his touch, responded as sweetly as she had before. Lizzie began lifting her hips, urging him deeper and deeper still when another orgasm claimed her. He sank fully inside her and almost lost it, too. He slid his hands beneath her bottom and pulled her closer while he stilled to savor the way she felt surrounding him, snug and hot and smooth as top-grade scotch. Paused in an effort to make it last.

"Jack," she whispered. "What's wrong?"

He nuzzled his face in her neck. "Nothing's wrong. It's just that you're so tight."

"Is that a bad thing?"

"It's a good thing. Too damn good."

She lifted his face into her palms. "Nothing can be too good."

Oh yeah, it could, Jack thought as he surrendered to his body's command, recognized the fact that he hadn't felt this great in a long time, if ever. Lizzie's gaze never strayed from his as he moved inside her with as much temperance as he could muster. It wasn't long until she caught on and moved with him, her eyes full of wide-eyed wonder but thankfully no hint of pain, only pleasure.

Too soon, Jack acknowledged when he could no longer hold his own climax at bay. Too, too soon.

The climax wracked his body and he shook with the explosion. As he tried to recover, Lizzie held him securely against her breasts and caressed his back with long, silken strokes.

"I never knew," she said in a reverent tone, bringing Jack back around to the here and now.

He kissed her as if he could never get enough of her. He marveled at the way she made love, relished her laughter, appreciated her zest for living.

In that moment Jack realized that the old saying about the road being paved with good intentions was patently true. He never intended to fall hard for any woman, much less Lizzie Matheson—a woman who had the capacity to creep past his reserve.

He couldn't forget that once this ordeal was over, he would still be the same old Jack with the same old shame, the same old failures. He would still have to deal with the life he had chosen and that didn't include making Lizzie a permanent part of it. He also knew that even after she left him alone, she would leave an indelible mark on his soul.

After drifting back to blissful sleep in Jack's arms, Lizzie awakened to find he'd disappeared again. She stretched her arms above her head and immediately realized it was much later than she'd first believed, evident by the sun's rays streaming into the deserted room.

She slipped from the bed and came to her feet on wooden legs that didn't seem to want to hold her weight. Otherwise, she felt remarkably well considering her recent activities. No real discomfort, now or before when Jack had made love to her. Oh, there had been some pain, but Jack's care, his gentleness, his fantastic skill had eased that quickly. She smiled over her good fortune in finding the consummate man to be her first lover. An incredible lover. A man she could so easily love. A man she already did love in many ways.

Lizzie took a few steps forward, thankful that the boat's movement had calmed considering that her memories of this morning made her feel anything but steady. She also felt sticky, both from the remnants of lovemaking and the salty rain that had adhered to her skin like plastic wrap. She wanted a bath, and she wanted food.

After retrieving one of Jack's T-shirts from the built-in bureau drawer, she put it on and headed to the kitchen, hoping to find Jack there. When she didn't, she assumed he was probably on deck checking things out. She would prefer that he check her out again.

Little did Jack know, he had created a supercharged, sexual need-machine. Even now, even though she was hungry enough to eat a live lobster, she would gladly forgo food for another bout of fun between the sheets.

But she had to remember her Hank. Hank needed food. Later she would deal with some kind of bath. Later she would deal with the melancholy emotions—the feelings for Jack crowding her heart, knowing Jack would probably never feel the same about her.

Lizzie opened one cabinet and took out a piece of bread—stale but luckily void of mold—and ate it with a small can of peaches and a bottle of water. Not a lot in the way of sustenance, but it would have to do until they made it back to shore. And when that happened, she would seek out a juicy hamburger—made from turkey, of course. She would have a real bath. She would have Jack one last time before they parted ways. If she couldn't have more, she would take what she could get.

Once she was finished eating, Lizzie took care of her morning routine then left the bathroom to find her stalwart sailor who had a knack for disappearing like a master magician.

When she arrived on deck, a little nip of self-consciousness bit into Lizzie as she shaded her eyes with her hand to search for Jack. What did one say the morning after? Actually, the afternoon after from the looks of the sun midpoint on the horizon. Nice day, Jack. Any sign of a rescue crew, Jack? Any chance I might convince you to go down below for some more slap and tickle?

Before she could come up with a more appropriate greeting, Lizzie pulled up short at the stern to find Jack on his knees at the swim platform, his bronzed skin shining in the sun. All of his skin. He was positioned at an angle profile to her, allowing Lizzie only a partial view of the details—half of his bare chest, one hair-covered thigh that hid attributes she now knew intimately. He had a bar of soap in one hand and a rag in the other and Lizzie had a case of the chills that paid no mind to the scorching heat.

She recognized that the boat was moving somewhat, a very good thing. She also recognized that she should turn away and give Jack some space, not just stand there like Lizzie the Vacationing Voyeur. But she felt as if her feet were stuck to the deck in wet cement. Her lips parted while she watched the play of his muscles and the drops of moisture as he ran the soapy rag over the back of his neck, down his sculpted chest, down his ridged abdomen to his... What she wouldn't give to be that rag.

He lowered his head, using the sea spray as a makeshift shower to wash his hair and to rinse. He straightened and slicked a hand over his scalp then turned his face toward the sun. After draping the rag on the side of a nearby bucket and tossing the soap in the container, he stood, giving Lizzie a firsthand peek at his first-rate bod. What a view.

But he didn't allow her enough time to enjoy the sight before he tugged on a pair of khaki shorts. He turned and hesitated when their gazes met, a knowing look gleaming in his silver eyes.

She'd definitely been caught, and she honestly didn't care. In fact, she was glad.

Lizzie raised her hand in a flat-palm wave, trying to appear nonchalant when she really wanted to tackle him. "Hi."

He favored her with a devastating half smile, his hand poised on his fly. "So you're finally awake."

She walked toward him, her hands clasped behind

her back so she wouldn't grab him without formality. "Yeah."

He slid his zipper up, slowly. "Are you feeling okay?"

"I feel great." Wired. Sexually keyed up. "I had some breakfast. I could definitely use a bath." She could definitely use a kiss, and more.

He pointed to the bucket. "There's some bottled water in there for you to use along with a sponge."

"What? No loofah?"

"Huh?"

"Never mind. A sponge is great."

"I brought the water out here to warm it. It's not much but it should be enough for you. You can take it back inside and bathe in there."

She nodded toward the platform. "I could do what you were doing."

"Believe me, Lizzie, salt water isn't that great."

She shrugged. "Okay." Lizzie reached for the hem of the tee to tug it off.

"Inside, Lizzie," Jack said in a warning tone. "You'll have more privacy."

Obviously he was much more courteous than she had been. But frankly, she didn't want to go inside. She didn't want Jack to leave, either. She wanted him to watch. She wanted him to be as affected as she'd been when she'd watched him.

Ignoring his suggestion, she pulled the shirt over her head, leaving her totally naked, and dropped it on the deck. "I've never bathed under the open skies before. It's kind of nice."

Jack didn't move, didn't speak as she soaped the

sponge and slid it down her body then back up to linger at her breasts. His gaze followed the rivulets of foamy moisture rolling down her belly and below.

He glanced up and she noted the unmistakable heat in his eyes. On a whim, she offered him the sponge. "Would you like to do it?"

He looked away. "Do you really think that's a good idea?"

She sauntered forward until she was standing before him, toe to toe. "I think it's a marvelous idea. I'm sure you'll do a very thorough job."

"I would think you might have other things on your mind."

"What other things?"

"Like when we're going to get out of here."

She lifted his hand and curled his fingers around the sponge. "No use worrying over what we can't control, right?"

He forked his free hand through his hair. "My control will be in jeopardy if I help you out with your bath."

"I certainly hope so."

"Lizzie, you're making me crazy."

She kissed his chin. "Jack, you're making me hot."

He reluctantly smiled. "No surprise. It's got to be over eighty degrees out here."

"That's not what I mean and you know it." She took his hand and guided the sponge to her breasts. "This is what I mean."

After lingering there for a time, he washed her belly then knelt and washed the inside of her thighs, her legs, each foot, before working his way back up, avoiding the place that begged for his attention. "How's that?"

"Not quite as thorough as I'd hoped."

"I really have something I need to do."

"I bet you do." She glanced at his fly. "Well, my, my. I believe J.J. is now present and accounted for."

"What do you expect when he has a beautiful, naked woman standing in front of him."

Lizzie was totally buoyed by the comment. "Beautiful, huh? Isn't that a stretch?"

He brushed her hair away from her face, looking seriously seductive. "You are beautiful." He tossed the sponge into the bucket and pulled her against him. "Incredibly beautiful." He outlined her lips with a fingertip. "Beautiful mouth." He lowered his hand to her breast and feathered her nipple with his thumb. "Beautiful here." He cupped the juncture of her thighs. "Definitely beautiful here."

Slanting his head, he kissed her deeply, touched her ardently until Lizzie feared her shaky limbs would give way. As if he sensed her predicament, he broke the kiss and took her hand, pulling her behind him toward the steps.

Lizzie planted her feet and yanked him around to kiss him again. She leaned back against the bulkhead and he followed, melding his mouth with hers, their tongues tangled in a dance of desperate desire.

She tried to work his fly, her fingers fumbling with the urgency to have him right then, right now. He pushed her hand away and she half expected him to

do the same to her. Instead, he lowered his zipper
and with one palm parted her legs, bent his knees
and thrust upward, seating himself deep inside her.
He kept his arm behind her back as a buffer against
the wall. Held her captive with the strength of his
body and a spellbinding kiss that didn't last long
enough.

"Lizzie," he whispered. "This isn't right."

"This is very right," she said as she slid her hands
beneath the back of his shorts to relish the play of
his muscled buttocks against her palms as he moved
in a steady cadence.

"I don't want to—"

"Hurt me, I know. You're not. You won't."

At least not physically, Lizzie's final coherent
thought as the delicious friction of Jack's body rub-
bing against hers sent her falling, falling toward a
sensual abyss where every nerve ending in her body
absorbed the sensations. Jack groaned with the next
thrust then went rigid in her arms as his own climax
took over.

When his ragged respiration began to settle, he
murmured, "This is insane," as he braced his palms
on either side of her head, taking his weight from
her, but not his body.

"This is heaven," Lizzie said.

They stayed that way for a time, a slight breeze
filtering over them as several gulls squawked overhead.

"Show's over," Lizzie called to the noisy birds.

Jack's laughter rumbled low in his chest as he
rolled away from her and leaned back against the

wall at her side. "Guess there's something to be said for being marooned."

She turned to her side and stared at his gorgeous face, his remarkable chest still glistening but this time from perspiration. Crazy as it seemed, she wanted him all over again. "You're so right. Just think, we can do it on a deck all we want without concern over getting caught." She tipped her face toward the soft blue skies. "Except maybe by a bird or two or ten."

Taking Lizzie by surprise, Jack tenderly stroked her cheek. She turned her gaze on him to find his expression almost regretful. "You deserve better than a deck, Lizzie. Better than up against a wall."

"I'm not complaining, Ahab."

"Neither am I. I'm just worried about—"

"I'm okay and Hank's okay." She pushed away from the wall. "Right now I need to finish my bath and you need to do whatever it is you need to do."

She headed back to the makeshift tub and snatched the shirt from the deck. After slipping it on, she picked up the bucket of water and turned to find Jack still reclining against the wall, watching her. He'd adjusted his shorts to the proper position but he still looked no less sexy to Lizzie. He did look very concerned.

She made her way over to him and smiled. "Don't look so serious. Everything's going to be okay. You're going to go about your business and I'm going to bathe by myself in the bathroom in case we're visited by pirates who are looking for booty. Both kinds."

Jack didn't smile but as she tried to pass by him to return below, he caught her palm and kissed it, halting her progress. "You're a remarkable woman, Lizzie. You deserve the best." He carried the weight of the world in his silver eyes, causing Lizzie's heart to clutch in her chest. If only she knew how to reach him, how to help him.

She stroked his shadowed jaw. "You deserve the best, too, Jack. You deserve some peace. I sincerely hope you find someone who'll give you that one day."

Even if I can't, Lizzie thought as she headed away. When she returned to the bathroom, she set down the bucket and sat on the edge of the tub. The bravado she'd been determined to show in Jack's presence dissolved and she gave in to unexpected tears.

Lizzie Matheson had only cried twice in her recent past—the day her father had died and the morning three days ago when she'd learned she was carrying a child. Lizzie had never cried over a man before, but then she'd never met anyone like Jackson Dunlap. She suspected these wouldn't be the last tears she shed over him. And for him.

Eight

Peace.

Jack had considered that he'd finally found some with Lizzie, if only temporarily. But when she wasn't around, the tranquility lifted and the guilt came calling again. He'd piled on some more remorse when he'd seen that look in her eyes, the one that told him she believed in him, that he really mattered. In reality, Lizzie mattered to Jack, too. A lot more than she should.

The ocean spread out before him, the weather much kinder this evening in some ways. Yet the sea seemed determined to keep them in suspended animation. He steered the boat in the direction of the shore, hoping the wind might pick up and drive them forward. The jib caught some of the breeze, but not enough to make much progress. They were running out of water, running out of food. Running out of time.

He wondered if Lizzie's friends had given up on her, if anyone even cared that he hadn't shown up at the resort to restock or gather his messages. Of course, he'd made it quite clear that he didn't want to be bothered, possibly to his own detriment. And Lizzie's. All he could do was hope that someone would come upon them soon.

The setting sun provided a kaleidoscope of color— varying shades of oranges and blues—and he considered calling Lizzie on deck to share the scene. But she'd been uncharacteristically quiet after dinner and he worried she was overly tired. He'd insisted she go to bed and promised he would join her later—a promise he wasn't sure he should keep. She was temptation encased in an irresistible body and if she got it in her head to test him again, he wouldn't be strong enough to resist her.

Jack continued to stand behind the wheel and absorb the sounds and smells—gulls flying overhead, the tangy scent of the sea, the waves lapping against the hull. For the first time in his life, he almost resented the atmosphere. Then another sound caught his attention. A boat motoring in the distance.

He squinted his eyes against the last light and saw the craft coming toward him. Unless he was totally off base, it looked like the same boat they'd encountered a day ago, piloted by the so-called fishermen, which could mean help had arrived—or they were in dire straits.

As the boat came closer, Jack verified it was the

suspicious pair. He gripped the wheel, mentally plotting what he would do if they had returned to search for valuables—and trouble. He had no ammunition but he did have the gun. They wouldn't know for certain it wasn't loaded. Unfortunately, the gun was locked away in the safe in the stateroom. He didn't trust leaving topsides and allowing them an opportunity to have the upper hand. And should they follow him, they would have access to Lizzie.

Lizzie was his main concern at the moment. He had to protect her, no matter what it took.

When they pulled alongside, Jack left the helm to confront the seedy strangers. The skinny one lifted a beer and said, "Guess you survived the storm."

Jack noticed all too late that the big one had moored the craft to the sailboat. He took on a casual stance that belied his concern. "We managed fine. I'm about to head back."

"I don't hear no motor," the big one said, followed by a grating laugh. "Do you hear a motor, Harry?"

"Nope, Buck, I don't hear no motor. I don't think this boat's going anywhere, at last not very fast."

Jack straightened, every nerve of his body sensing danger. "No fish today, gentlemen?"

Emaciated Harry rubbed his scratchy jaw. "We're not fishing today. Not that kind of fishing anyway. Where's your wife?"

"She's gone," Jack lied. "Went back to shore with another boat. Coast Guard should be by any time now."

"Did you see any Coast Guard on the way out, Buck?"

"Nope, Harry. I figure the Coast Guard has more important things to do than worry about stranded honeymooners."

Jack's mind whirled when he saw Buck reach into his pocket. "What do you two want?"

As suspected, Buck pulled out a revolver, dwarfed in his beefy palm. "We want to see what you got hiding on that boat there."

Jack gritted his teeth and spoke through them. "I don't have a damn thing you'd want."

"You're wrong about that." Buck climbed aboard and Jack started forward until he heard the cock of the gun. "Don't move, Cap'n. Now just ease on back and let us take a look around."

Jack stood helplessly by while the other reprobate joined them on deck. He couldn't protect Lizzie if they shot him. Maybe they'd just take what they wanted and get the hell out of there.

He considered trying to negotiate, something he was damn good at when it came to business. But he doubted he could reason with two smugglers who had the combined intelligence of a grouper.

Buck handed the gun to Harry, a good thing, Jack decided, since Harry was half his size. If presented the opportunity, Jack could overpower him. But not yet. Not until the time was right.

"Well, looky here," Buck said, kneeling beside the railing. He came up clutching something in his hand and when he dangled it before them, Jack realized it was Lizzie's good-luck charms. He hoped like hell they worked now.

Harry aimed the gun at Jack's chest. "Any other treasure out here?"

"No."

"Take a look around, Buck," Harry said. "I'll take the captain here down below and see what else we can find. Pick up anything that's not tied down."

"Sure thing, Harry."

"Turn around, Capt'n, and walk," Harry said.

Jack complied and felt the barrel of the gun at his back. He started down the steps slowly, praying Lizzie was still tucked away in bed.

"You gotta safe on board?" Harry asked as they descended the steps.

Jack thought about lying then considered that if he handed over the cash, the guy might be satisfied. But the safe was sequestered in the floor of the stateroom closet, the same room containing Lizzie. Could he take that chance? Maybe if he spoke loud enough, warned her in advance, she could find a place to hide and hopefully not in the closet. He had to believe she would understand what was taking place.

The main salon was practically dark due to the hour, something that could work to his and Lizzie's advantage.

"Right this way, Harry," Jack said in an overly loud, sarcastic voice. "It's in the stateroom. Will hundreds be okay or do you prefer smaller bills?"

"Money's money."

"Have you guys ever thought about an honest job?

I hear they could use someone to clean the heads back in Key Largo.''

The gun bit into Jack's back. "No time to be funny, Capt'n. I've killed people for a lot less.''

That provided little comfort for Jack as he opened the stateroom door. Like the salon, the room was dimly lit. Jack immediately homed in on the bed, thankful to find it deserted.

Good girl, Lizzie.

Turning to his right, Jack blindly worked his way to the closet and pulled open the doors. "I can't see anything, Harry. The battery's down so I don't have any lights.''

"No problem.''

Jack heard the snap of a flashlight and the beam angled onto the floor, revealing the safe. Maybe Buck and Harry weren't so stupid after all.

Jack knelt and worked the combination, opened the door, pulled out the only two bundles of cash and handed it over his shoulder.

"Give me that gun,'' Harry demanded. "And no funny stuff. I'll shoot you right here.''

Jack handed the weapon over to Harry then straightened and faced him. The guy looked more menacing in the scarce light with his fried hair sticking out of the dirty white cap, his lips curled into a smile that displayed a definite lack of dental hygiene. Jack would be more than happy to remove the rest of his teeth. But first, he had to get out of the cabin.

"I have a few other trinkets that might interest you in the salon,'' Jack said.

"Lead the way, Capt'n.''

Jack exited the stateroom expecting to find Buck waiting for them but the cabin was deserted. He hoped Lizzie stayed back, stayed hidden and didn't do something totally inadvisable like try to conduct her own rescue.

"I've got some silver in the galley," Jack said.

When they passed by the companionway, a loud noise from above shook the walls. No telling what Buck was up to. Jack hoped he'd slipped and landed flat on his back.

Harry leaned over and yelled up the steps, "What are you doing, you fool?"

The pressure of the gun released from Jack's back and he saw his chance. He whirled around and knocked it from Harry's grasp then took him down onto the ground. They rolled into the middle of the salon and Jack managed to have Harry pinned in a matter of moments.

He rammed his forearm against Harry's throat. "Not so tough without the weapon, are you, my friend."

"Buck's gonna kill you with his bare hands," Harry choked out.

Not if Jack could find the gun. He kept his knee planted in Harry's concave chest and groped for the weapon. The flashlight had rolled away and lodged at the corner of the sofa. Footsteps on the stairs increased his urgency. When Harry tried to move, Jack wrapped his hands around his neck.

Where was the damn gun?

"Looking for this?"

Jack glanced up to see Buck's hulking figure at

the bottom of the companionway, the gun trained on Jack's head.

"Let him up," Buck hissed. "Then lie face-down."

Bile rose in Jack's throat when he realized he was outnumbered. He wouldn't be able to protect Lizzie because in a few minutes, most likely he would be dead.

He wasn't afraid of dying; he never had been. But he was afraid for Lizzie. Again he would fail another woman, only this one meant more to him than he could express.

Buck moved closer, hovering above them. "I said turn him loose."

Jack was tempted to crush Harry's larynx and he could with the fury he felt. Before he could answer Buck's command, a sickening crack echoed in the room and Buck slumped to the ground in a huge heap.

"Take that, you ugly blowfish."

Jack's brain took a moment to register the sight of Lizzie standing over Buck, the doorstop trophy clutched in her grip. She crouched and set it down then picked up the gun in trembling fingers, aiming it at Buck who remained motionless.

Jack held out his open palm. "Give it here."

Lizzie handed off the gun to Jack and snatched the flashlight, shining the beam on Buck. "Oh, God. Did I kill him?"

Jack straightened and pointed the revolver at Harry. Harry moaned and so did Buck. "He's not dead but I'll wager he'll have one hell of a headache in the morning." He centered his gaze on Harry. "If I decide to let him and his buddy live."

Harry lifted his arms above his head and whined, "Don't shoot me, man. It was all Buck's idea."

Jack glanced at Lizzie. "What do you think, Dorothy? Should I let them live?"

Lizzie's smile illuminated the room. "You could shoot them in a place that would make them sing falsetto, although it's probably a small target."

Harry's hands went to his crotch and Lizzie and Jack shared in a laugh.

"Guess we should find something to tie them up," Lizzie said then walked to the windows and pulled the tiebacks from the curtains. "This will do for now."

"Good thinking, Dorothy." Jack's tone was laced with humor but his heart was full of relief. Lizzie was damned smart. Most important, Lizzie was safe.

Lizzie sat on the sofa in the main salon lit by the lone lantern. She couldn't seem to rid herself of chills even though she was covered in all her clothes and a blanket. Jack was on deck talking to the Coast Guard who had shown up an hour before, after he'd called for help from the dirty duo's boat. They'd carted the pair away and now Lizzie awaited Jack's return and information on what would happen next.

The ordeal was over. That should have pleased Lizzie and it did in a way. She would be back on land soon. She and Hank were okay. She could call and let everyone know she had survived. But it also meant her time with Jack was coming to an end.

She heard someone descending the steps and her heart took flight when Jack appeared. He joined her on the couch and wrapped one arm around her shoulders.

"You took a big chance tonight, Lizzie."

She shrugged. "I didn't have a choice. I refused to let those idiots have their way."

Jack shifted to face her and took her hands. "I don't understand how you got past us and into the head."

She sent him a sheepish smile. "Actually, I was in the head, shaving my legs."

He tried to look stern but amusement glinted in his eyes. "With my razor?"

"Sorry. I forgot to pack my toiletries for the trip."

"I suppose I can forgive you this time since you basically saved our lives."

But can you forgive yourself? The thought bolted into Lizzie's brain and she almost voiced it. Almost. "Anyway, I was heading out when I heard you talking to dear Harry. I decided to stay put for a while to figure out what to do. Then I remembered the trophy. It came in handy but it's a lot heavier than I'd realized."

He kissed her forehead. "And you are a lot more resourceful than I'd realized."

She saluted. "All in a day's work, Captain."

The roar of an engine filtered down from above. Lizzie couldn't count how many times she'd prayed to hear that welcome sound over the past few days. Now it only made her sad.

"I believe our ride's waiting," Jack said, his gaze fastened on hers.

"Guess this is it," Lizzie answered, trying to keep the gloom from her voice. "The end of the yellow brick road, so to speak."

"Actually, I've arranged for someone to tow the boat and for us to spend the night in Key Largo. I'll have someone take you back to Miami tomorrow."

Tomorrow. Lizzie wasn't looking forward to what tomorrow would bring—the end of her time with Jack. But they still had tonight. "Where exactly are you taking me?"

He came to his feet and held out his hands. "Just this little place I know."

Little was anything but an appropriate description of the Twelve Sands Resort. Lizzie couldn't believe that her first night back on land would include a stay-over at a place fit for a goddess.

As they walked through the massive marble-and-gold lobby, Lizzie felt like a washed up rodent in her disheveled clothes and stringy hair, her skin sporting a fine covering of salt. When a debonair, silver-haired gentleman wearing a neatly pressed suit approached her and Jack, she considered ducking behind the palm tree to her right. Not that it would provide much cover.

He held out his hand to Jack. "Mr. Dunlap, this is certainly a nice surprise."

Jack shook the man's hand while Lizzie mentally chanted, *Don't introduce me, don't intro—*

"Mr. Brevard, this is Elizabeth Matheson, my guest for the evening."

The man sent her a welcoming smile as if she were royalty, not ragged. "So happy to have you, Ms. Matheson." He turned his attention back to Jack. "We have the suite ready. I'll have someone bring you your messages. What else do you require?"

"Have room service prepare me my usual," Jack said. "Ms. Matheson will require a vegetarian meal."

"Champagne?" Brevard asked.

Jack glanced at Lizzie then said, "No champagne tonight. Just plenty of water."

"Very good, sir."

Jack regarded Lizzie. "Anything else, Dorothy?"

Lizzie immediately noted the hint of surprise in Brevard's expression before he returned to the business facade. More than likely, he assumed they were having a tryst and Jack accidentally called her by her real name.

"Actually, Ahab, I'd really like a hot fudge sundae."

"I'm sure that can be arranged," Jack said.

"Most certainly," Brevard answered, still looking more than a little confounded.

"And I need foam pillows, if that's okay," Lizzie said. "I'm a little allergic to feathers."

Jack placed a hand on her back as if to nudge her forward. She was probably pushing her luck but she had one more request. "Would you happen to have a Miami phone book, Mr. Brevard?"

"Of course. I'll have everything sent right up."

She gave him her sunniest smile. "Great. I have a few calls to make."

"And Mr. Brevard," Jack said. "Could you please arrange for Dr. Jacobs to come to the suite within the hour?"

Brevard's expression went from confused to concerned. "Are you ill, sir?"

"I would like for him to examine Ms. Matheson."

Lizzie stared at Jack. "That's really not necessary. I'm sure the baby is fine."

Brevard cleared his throat. "Will that be all?"

Jack looked more than chagrined. "Yes, that will be all."

He took Lizzie by the elbow and guided her through the lobby and into an elevator made of glass on three sides. They were the only two occupants, a good thing because Lizzie had plenty to say. "I can wait to see my own doctor, Jack. When I get back to Miami, I'll make an appointment."

"I'd feel better knowing you're okay before you leave. As soon as the boat's repaired, I'll be heading back out."

Back out to sea, back out of her life. "I'm sure everything is A-okay with Hank." She patted her belly. "Considering he's floating around all the time, I doubt he even noticed we were on a boat."

"I'm sure you're right, but humor me, okay?"

She rolled her eyes. "Okay, if I must."

The doors opened on the fourth floor and a young couple entered the car. Most likely a pair of newly-weds, Lizzie decided, considering the way they clung to each other like human moss and exchanged glances along with the occasional kiss. She and Jack stood on opposite sides of the elevator, pretending not to notice. But Lizzie noticed even though she tried with all her might not to.

Feeling somewhat down in the dumps, Lizzie turned to stare out the glass enclosure as they climbed upward. Under normal circumstances, she would appreciate the view of the indoor maze of water gardens zigzagging across the lobby and the bronze statue of dolphins—a honeymooners' paradise. But she and Jack weren't on their honeymoon. Not even close. They were preparing for an ending, not a new beginning.

The couple followed Jack and Lizzie into the foyer of the top floor where the honeymooners entered an exclusive-looking restaurant emitting luscious smells that made Lizzie's stomach groan like a rusty tailpipe. Surely Jack didn't intend for them to stop off for a meal. She was wearing the same set of clothes she'd worn the day she'd dropped in on Jack, along with a pair of his deck shoes, not at all suitable for a place that most likely adhered to a dress code.

Fortunately, Jack told her, "This way," and led her through an ornate corridor with rich-blue carpets and lots of mirrors that Lizzie purposely avoided. If she got a good gander at herself, she would definitely be depressed.

All she wanted right now was a long shower and to gorge on a decent meal then crawl between the sheets, preferably with Jack. But that remained to be seen. Would they have one last night together? Or was this it?

So long, Lizzie. It's been interesting, Lizzie. Good-bye, Lizzie.

They came to an alcove hidden in the corner behind two large plants sporting lovely orange and red flowers. Jack used a card key to access the elevator and they both stepped inside. Obviously they hadn't been at the top of the high-rise after all, Lizzie realized when they traveled one more floor.

The elevator opened to a set of double doors, which Jack used the same key to unlock. Jack pushed the doors open and Lizzie entered a luxurious foyer straight out of the movies, all gilt and marble, much like the lobby. Beyond that, a penthouse suite straight out of a dream. She resisted the urge to kick off the too-big shoes and curl her toes into the white carpet, not at all a good idea.

One whole wall was tinted glass, revealing a multitude of stars and tiny twinkling lights coming from the harbor below. The designer furniture carried out a nautical theme with shades of blue and touches of red, an apt reflection of the typical luxury seaside resort. Jack stood by looking pleased and peacock-proud, as if he'd just discovered hidden treasure.

Slowly Lizzie turned around to survey the room. "Wow."

"I take it you like the accommodations?"

Her gaze zipped to his. "Like them? I've never, ever stayed in any place so…so…rich."

"Good. Make yourself comfortable."

Lizzie didn't dare sit on the furniture, not until she was clean. "You must stay here often considering the fact everyone knew you downstairs."

"I live here, when I'm not on the boat."

Holy mackerel. "You live in a resort? That must cost a fortune."

He forked a hand through his hair. "Actually, it doesn't cost me a thing. I own the place."

"They let you buy the penthouse?"

His grin reappeared. "I own the whole resort. This one, and five others throughout the world."

Lizzie swallowed hard. Granted, she suspected Jack had a good deal of money from the looks of the yacht. But she had no idea that she'd spent the past few days keeping company—and making whoopee— with a tycoon. "Well, Ahab, looks like you've done pretty well."

"I do okay."

Okay? If this resort denoted only okay, she would love to see his idea of great. "So what now?"

The question seemed to hang on the air for a long moment until he said, "I personally would like to take a shower." He pointed to Lizzie's right. "The bathroom's through there. You'll find a robe hanging in the closet."

"Really, Jack, I don't mind if you go first."

He gestured to his left. "My bedroom and bath is down there. Yours is in the guest suite."

Oh, so she had been relegated to guest status. So much for their final night together. "Great. I'll just take a shower now."

"Good. Dr. Jacobs should be up within the hour."

"I won't take long."

"Take your time. He can wait awhile. I keep him

on the hotel payroll and supply him with plenty of free golf, so he's always very accommodating.''

Lizzie wished she could say the same for Jack, not that he hadn't been very accommodating to this point. But it looked as if that might all be over. ''Fine. See you in a bit.''

Lizzie wandered down the small hallway and opened another set of double doors to another room fit for royalty. But this one had a more classic decor, almost feminine in some ways with its cool Caribbean colors, a peach-and-turquoise comforter covering the queen-size bed. Maybe Jack entertained a lot of female guests. If that were true, she doubted they would require their own bedroom since she was certain they shared Jack's bed. And that thought made her seethe.

How stupid for her to be jealous, she thought as she stripped out of her icky clothes and made her way into the fabulous peach-colored bath. Whatever had existed between her and the captain was basically over. That didn't make her any less disappointed. That didn't make her want him any less. Or love him any less. And she did love him even knowing he could never love her back.

As she washed away the remnants of the sea, she felt as if she were washing away the last vestiges of Jack's kisses, Jack's touch, Jack's incredible care.

But she knew in her heart that she would never, ever wash away the memories. If she couldn't have Jack, she would always have those.

Nine

Jack paced outside the guest quarters while Dr. Henry Jacobs examined Lizzie, thinking it odd that he felt so nervous, felt as if he were an anxious father. That thought stopped him cold.

He wasn't the father of Lizzie's baby. He wasn't responsible for them from this point forward. But he wasn't sure he would ever stop feeling responsible, especially if the exam resulted in bad news.

Jack moved a little closer to the closed doors and heard both Lizzie and Jacobs laughing. Jacobs rarely laughed. In fact, he'd been known to hurl a club or two or three on the golf course even if he was kicking everyone's butt. But then Lizzie would probably have a doomed man guffawing as he headed to the gallows.

The doorknob turned and Jack stepped back, but

not quite quickly enough to hide the fact he'd been eavesdropping.

After closing the door behind him, Jacobs approached Jack and patted him on the back. "She's one healthy lady."

"Are you sure? The baby—"

"Looks okay, but it's hard to tell since she's in her first trimester. I told Lizzie she needed to check in with her OB for a more thorough exam, but if something had happened, she would have known by now."

"Okay. If you're sure."

"Yeah, I'm sure, so don't look so damn worried."

Jack glanced over Jacobs's head toward the doors. "Where is she?"

"Getting dressed."

As asinine as it seemed, Jack was jealous that Lizzie had undressed for Henry Jacobs, a short, balding sixtyish semiretired doctor who had a paunchy middle and a wife of thirty-something years.

"I appreciate you taking care of her," Jack said.

"Not a problem. Make sure she drinks plenty of liquids. And don't whisk her away on any lengthy boat rides for a week or two and she'll be fine. Other than that, carry on as usual."

"Is that okay? I mean, the carrying-on bit." Now why the hell had he asked that? He didn't plan to make love to Lizzie again. She was leaving tomorrow. That would complicate everything. She needed her rest. She didn't need him.

Jacobs chuckled. "If you're asking me if it's okay to have a little activity between the sheets, as far as the pregnancy's concerned, I see no harm in that at all. Lizzie can let you know if it's a problem.''

Jack headed to the door with Jacobs following behind him. Before the doctor left, he faced Jack with his usual staid expression. ''Take care of your girl. She's a very special lady. And congratulations. About time you decided to settle down.''

Your girl...

Jack was preparing a rebuttal when he heard approaching footsteps behind him. Then Jacobs raised his hand in a wave and said, ''Good night, Lizzie. It's been a pleasure.''

Jack still hadn't voiced a denial when Jacobs headed out the door. He turned to Lizzie and found her standing in the room, looking somewhat sheepish. ''He thinks this is my baby?''

She tightened the sash on the terry robe. ''I swear I had no idea he would make the wrong assumption. He didn't ask the hows or whys about the baby, just questions about the pregnancy. Did you know he has five kids?''

Jack only knew one thing, he needed to set the record straight with Jacobs as soon as possible. The man wasn't only a practiced golfer, he was an expert gossip, at least when it came to the goings-on at the resort. By noon tomorrow everyone would learn that Jack was going to be a father. People would be shaking his hands and congratulating him. He would have to endure comments about having his own little sailor. Of course, then he'd be expected to pass out cigars and talk about which university his boy would attend. He would insist on Florida State, his alma mater. He'd definitely encourage him to consider something steady, like business, so he could run the company one day and...

Jack threw on the mental brakes.

Tomorrow she would be gone. No more Lizzie or Hank in his life. No more hearing her laughter, or listening to her bad jokes. No more waking up next to her. And that was for the best. Then where did that nagging ache in his chest come from?

Probably a lack of decent food.

Jack gestured toward the dining-room table. "Dinner is served. Let's eat before it gets cold."

Before he did something stupid, like ask her to be his girl, permanently.

After contacting the head of the chase crew, who'd been elated to learn she hadn't met a watery end, Lizzie consumed her dinner like a field hand, eating every last bit of the vegetarian lasagna, salad and sundae. At this rate she would have to be transported by heavy-duty equipment at the end of seven months. Seven months that she would spend alone until the birth of her precious baby.

But she wouldn't think about that now. She would concentrate on the few hours remaining with Jack.

Solemn Jack, who had pushed his half-eaten dinner away and sat silently staring into space, a far-off look in his eyes. Lizzie assumed he was already considering returning to sea. More than likely, he would be happy to be rid of her. But she wasn't going anywhere until morning. They still had one last night together, and she intended to make the most of it, if he cooperated.

Lizzie leaned back in her chair, crossed her hands over her tummy and sighed. "Dollar for your thoughts."

He smiled but it looked almost sad. "Isn't that supposed to be a penny for my thoughts?"

Lizzie returned his smile. "Not at today's rate of inflation. But since I don't have any spare change, I guess I can't even offer you a penny." She could offer him her body but decided to move slowly lest he decide to make a quick getaway.

She rested her cheek on her palm. "What has you in such a melancholy mood? That old wanderlust?"

His smile faded, giving way to a serious expression. "I was thinking about you going home tomorrow."

Did she dare hope that he was going to miss her? That he might ask her to stay? Probably not. But maybe he would want to see her again. "What about it?"

"What are you going to do for money?"

Of course. Millionaires thought a lot about money. Jack was a millionaire. Probably a multimillionaire. Jack was also a loner. He had no intention of ever seeing her again. And she had no intention of accepting a handout, if that's what he was offering. "I'm going to get my old job back at the day spa. I should be able to add to my savings since the balloon was insured. Hank and I will be just fine."

"Let me buy you a new balloon," he said.

Great. A parting gift. "That's not necessary."

"I insist."

"I'll buy another one someday." But she doubted she would ever find a man like Jack—a lonely successful sailor searching for a tranquillity not quite within his reach. The consummate lover. And beneath the stoic facade, a caring man.

"I wish you would at least consider it," he said. "After all, I'm the one who put Bessie out of commission."

"After I practically destroyed *Hannah*."

This time his smile was brighter. "We've been through a lot together, haven't we, Liz?"

Lizzie's heart clutched in her chest. "What did you call me?"

He frowned. "Liz. Is that a problem?"

"No." Lizzie bit the inside of her cheek to stop the threatening tears. "My dad used to call me that because he thought it sounded more grown-up. Of course, the first time he said it, I was only ten and I had just beaten up the bully next door. I pretty much knew I was in trouble."

"I assure you, you're not in trouble now."

Lizzie saw her chance and decided to take it. "Oh, darn. I was kind of hoping I was."

Jack leaned forward. "In what way?"

She stood and approached him, bolstering her courage, expecting a possible rejection. "I was hoping for the kind of trouble dealt out by a sexy sailor who is very hard to resist." She braced her hands on his shoulders from behind and leaned to kiss his cheek.

He laid his hands on hers but didn't turn around. "You'll be leaving tomorrow."

Like he really had to remind her of that. "I know."

He rose from the chair and faced her, standing so close that she could get the full effect of his sea-breeze cologne and his penetrating silver eyes. "I imagine you're tired."

"Not that tired."

He was dressed in business casual and she was wearing nothing but a hospitality robe. That could easily be remedied. She began to unbutton his tailored white shirt, gathering all the arguments should he try to stop her. But he didn't. He continued to watch her, his hands at his sides, while she parted the fabric to reveal his solid chest. Lizzie looked her fill knowing that it might be the last time. She stored the vision of his bronzed skin and tensile muscle in her mind, something to bring out on a rainy day. Her own little ray of sunshine. But she wasn't quite done taking mental pictures.

When she reached for Jack's belt, he muttered, "Not this time."

Lizzie opened her mouth in protest, only to have it closed by Jack's lips covering hers in a star-producing kiss. The earth fell away from beneath her as he continued to gently explore with his soft, heavenly tongue. Then she realized Jack was lifting her into his arms, carrying her away in every sense. She opened her eyes when she heard a door close behind them.

Jack broke the kiss and slid her down along the

length of him then framed her face in his palms. "Are you sure about this?"

She nodded.

"It's only tonight, Lizzie. I have to—"

She stopped his words with a brief kiss. "I know what you have to do, and what I have to do. You have to find your way, and I have to find mine. But we still have tonight."

Stepping back, she undid the sash at her waist and let the robe fall to her feet. Even as Jack's gaze roamed over her body in a leisurely exploration, even though she was totally exposed emotionally and physically, she didn't feel the least bit self-conscious by his perusal. This was Jack, a man whom she had only known a brief time, yet she felt as though she'd known him forever. If only she could know him forever after.

She'd never had a doubt about the existence of his heart, especially now when she saw it shining in his eyes, in his words when he said, "I don't believe I've ever met a more beautiful woman, inside and out."

A lump formed in Lizzie's throat, blocking any response. She fought back the tears, a war she was determined to win, at least tonight. Tomorrow she could mourn. Tomorrow she could cry. Tonight she would simply love. Love Jack with all that she had to give.

Jack removed his own clothes while she watched then held out his hand. He guided her down on the bed covered in blue satin sheets, then guided her into pure rapture when he sent his hands, his mouth, on a thorough excursion over her flushed body. She did the same to him, memorizing every detail from the bend of his elbow to the birthmark on his thigh—and every magnificent part in between.

He slid inside her on a sigh, and she came apart on a moan. The time they had spent together over the past few days seemed to come down to this moment—bodies twined in pleasure, a sensual stirring, an incredible jolt to the senses, an experience that Lizzie would never forget.

And she would never forget how he folded her in his arms in the aftermath, how he stroked her hair in silence and kissed her cheek as if she were a gift. Never would forget how much she loved him.

She would take that with her when she left tomorrow, along with her memories of a man who had no idea how much he had to give, if only he would forgive himself.

Jack stayed awake to watch Lizzie sleep in the glow of the bedside lamp that he'd intentionally left on. She smiled now and then, as if she was keeping a secret. He had more than a few secrets of his own, or he had until he'd met her. Never before had he revealed so much of himself to a woman. To anyone, for that matter.

Lizzie had a way of making him want to confess all his sins and ask for absolution. Had a way of making him want to be a better man. She also brought out his protective side. But Lizzie didn't need his protection; she'd proved that to him on more than one occasion. She did need a man who could give all of himself to her, to be a father for her baby. Jack had buried a good deal of his heart at sea. He wasn't sure he would ever be able to recover the part of him he'd sufficiently shrouded in shame.

Yes, Lizzie now knew his secrets, and it hadn't seemed to matter to her at all that he was anything but perfect. Still, she needed more than he was capable of giving, at least at this point in his life.

Yet he still had one more secret she would never know, and that was for the best.

He loved her, and he probably always would, even after she disappeared from his life.

The day was bright and sunny, but a tempest was gathering force in Lizzie's heart. As she stood beside the hotel limousine Jack had arranged to take her back to the mainland, she managed to force a smile despite the fact she felt like sobbing.

Taking a moment to push back the emotions, she stared out over the harbor and noticed Jack's boat had been towed into port. She'd been surprised he'd agreed to leave it and return in the Coast Guard cutter with her. He had said he wanted to make certain she was safe. Just one more thing she loved about him, the way he had been so determined to keep her and Hank protected.

While Jack spoke with the driver, a bellman approached Lizzie and asked, "Do you have luggage, ma'am?"

"Just this. I'm traveling kind of light this trip." She handed him the bag housing her old clothing. That morning she'd awakened to a box containing the sleeveless teal dress she now wore, along with a pair of matching sandals. Jack had told her that he'd sent his assistant to the hotel's exclusive boutique to select the correct size, but he'd insisted on the color since it matched her eyes.

Overcome by gratitude, she'd engaged him in a voracious hug and that turned into another round of uncontrollable passion. More memories made along with more sweet, sweet love.

And now they were about to say goodbye. An inevitable moment, one that was coming too soon.

Jack approached her, his hands buried in his pockets, admiration on his face as he gave her a long once-over. "You look great."

So did he in his navy jacket, khaki slacks and white tailored shirt, Lizzie thought. Every inch the prosperous, handsome businessman. A wealthy, dynamic man who could have his choice of any woman. She didn't want to consider that now.

Lizzie smoothed a hand over the dress. "Thanks again for this. I'm glad I'll have a chance to wear it before it doesn't fit any longer."

He studied the asphalt as if it was too painful to look at her. "Be sure to call me when the baby's born."

"I've been thinking about that," she said, and she had, a lot last night and this morning. "I'd like to ask you something. A favor, really."

He stared at her with a hint of alarm. "What?"

She playfully punched him in the arm. "Don't look so worried. I'm not going to ask you to play daddy."

"Oh."

"But I would like you to consider being Hank's godfather."

His laugh was gruff, cynical. "You could do better than me, Lizzie."

"Give yourself some credit, Jack. I would love to have you as a role model for Hank. You're a good man."

He hesitated for a moment. "You're going to be a great mom, and I'll think about it."

Lizzie wanted to shout with glee. "Good. And if you ever decide you want a friend, give me a call. I'm in the book."

"I will."

Lizzie doubted he would, but she could always hope. "Do you have any family nearby?"

He lowered his head and rubbed his nape. "No family to speak of. Both my parents are gone and have been for a number of years."

So they had something in common after all. "I really hate the fact that you're alone."

"As I've said before, I don't mind—"

"Being alone," Lizzie finished. "I know. But it's not as much fun as having someone around to harass. I'm really going to miss that with us."

Finally, he smiled. "Yeah, and I'm going to miss having my very own hairstylist on board. Guess I'll just let the hair grow."

"And the next time I see you, I'll call you Rip instead of Ahab."

When Jack didn't respond, when he failed to acknowledge that they would see each other again,

Lizzie gripped the car's door handle and said, "Okay, then. I guess I better get going so you can get back to work, or whatever it is you plan to do."

"First, I plan to do this." He pulled her hand from the limo then pulled her against him for a gentle yet thorough kiss. "I'll never forget you, Dorothy."

For good measure, Lizzie grabbed his butt. "I'm gonna miss you and J.J."

His grin reappeared. "I'm sure J.J. will miss you, too."

But will you? Lizzie wanted to ask. Instead, she opened the car door and slid inside. No use prolonging the inevitable. Besides, she could easily cry a gully-washer if he kept looking at her with those soulful silver eyes, like a lost little boy who had no real direction.

She had always been drawn to strays, from dogs to people. But Jack wasn't a stray, he was simply suffering from the cruel hand of fate. She couldn't save him from a meaningless existence. That was totally up to him.

Jack closed the door, closing the chapter on Ahab and Dorothy, a story that had the makings of a real-life fairy tale, except for one thing. No happy ending.

Lizzie knew that if she didn't tell him now, before the chance slipped away, she would always wonder if it might have made a difference. Most likely not, but her father had told her to aim at honesty and shoot straight, and that regrets were to be avoided at all costs.

She rolled down the window and crooked her finger at Jack. He crouched by the door and she leaned over, wrapped her arms around his neck then drew in a breath. "Promise me something, Jack."

"Okay."

"Promise to rejoin the land of the living. It's high time you forgive yourself."

"I'll try."

"Good." *Just do it, Lizzie.*

She brushed a lock of hair from his forehead, pulled him forward and whispered in his ear, "Even if I'd known it would turn out like this, I would have loved you anyway."

With that she let him go, gave him a smile, closed the window and told the driver, "You can go now."

She waved at Jack who stood with his hands in his pockets, his eyes locked with hers until the limo turned away and headed toward the road to home. Away from Jack.

Although her declaration might not have meant anything to him, it had meant everything to her.

Now she had no regrets except one—tomorrow she would wake without him in her life.

Ten

After packing provisions that would last at least a month, Jack set out on the newly restored *Hannah* alone.

As he'd promised Lizzie, he'd attempted to rejoin the living over the past two months. He'd met with colleagues, attended a couple of social events and even played a few rounds of golf. But he felt no more alive for the effort, the reason why he'd turned to his haven once more.

The Florida weather was crisp and clear, unseasonably cool for mid-August with only moderate winds. A good day for sailing, Jack thought as he guided his boat through the expanse of endless ocean. But regardless of the favorable conditions and the fact he'd been out for only a couple of hours, the atmosphere was starting to get to him—the salt, the sea air, the solitude.

A few miles from port, Jack set the sails and the course, turned on the autopilot, went down below and collapsed onto the sofa. Reaching into his pocket, he withdrew the necklace he'd inadvertently torn from Lizzie during the storm and held it in his palm. The police had recovered it from the smugglers and sent it by courier to the hotel that morning.

Now Jack had possession of something that should be in the hands of its rightful owner—even though he was tempted to keep it as a reminder of his and Lizzie's time together. But that wouldn't be fair since she had coveted her good-luck charms.

He could mail it to her, but then he would risk having it lost in transit. He should give it to her in person.

Why not? He could see how she was doing, make sure Hank was okay. He only had to stay long enough to hand over the necklace, and see her smile one more time.

Who was he trying to fool? If he saw her again, he would be tempted to take her into his arms, to make love to her for hours, for days. Right now he wasn't certain she would even want to see him again.

But God, he missed her.

After setting the necklace on the galley counter, Jack paced the length of the boat, his footsteps echoing in the silence as he wandered from cabin to cabin. The place looked in order, the perfect home away from home—or it had been at one time. Now everything served as a reminder of how he had spent his life in a safe shell. How he had tried to escape his responsibilities, the guilt—and he hadn't been successful. He couldn't escape the memories of Lizzie, either.

Even though the yacht's interior had been redone and the facade had changed dramatically, everywhere he looked he saw her. Saw her at the table, playing a hand of poker, pretending she didn't have a clue. Saw her in his bunk on her back, naked, her arms outstretched in welcome. He heard her laughter, heard her endless, endearing banter. And then he heard the words he hadn't wanted to heed.

I would have loved you anyway...

Lizzie loved him, and he didn't understand why. Maybe she'd been grateful to him for keeping her safe. Maybe it had to do with their intimacy. Maybe for once in his life, someone actually loved him for who he was, not what he could offer from a monetary standpoint. But could he give Lizzie what she needed?

He honestly didn't know. For that reason, he should stay out of her life, even if he did love her, too. Even if he hurt like hell when he thought about never seeing her again.

The shrill of the cell phone jerked Jack back into reality. He sent a litany of curses directed at modern communication and the fact he wasn't far enough out to lose the signal. Of course, he didn't have to do anything but ignore it. Yet for reasons he couldn't quite explain, he chose to answer the call.

And by the time the conversation ended, Jack was damned glad he had.

* * *

"Lizzie, you have a client waiting."

Glancing at her watch, Lizzie released an audible groan and glared at the salon's receptionist who wore her makeup like war paint. "It's Saturday, Penney. I'm supposed to be off by noon and it's almost three. Can't someone else do it?"

The woman stuck a pencil behind her ear and molded her devil-red lips into a fake grin. "Actually, I asked him that, but he refused. Besides, everyone else is completely booked."

Great. Lizzie pushed her fist into the small of her back that ached like a sore tooth. Hank was growing at an astounding rate, and obviously bent on reminding her often of his presence. "Oh, all right. But this is it. I'm starving." She surveyed the waiting room yet found it full of only women and children, not one male in sight. "Where is he?"

"He's at the shampoo bowl. Lila took care of that. Now he's all yours."

"What's his name?"

"I don't know."

"Didn't you ask?"

Penney rolled her chartreuse-shadowed eyes to the ceiling and patted her bottle-red big hair. "Of course I asked, but he wouldn't say anything except that you've cut his hair before. You can't miss him since he's the only client back there. And he's really good-looking, I might add. Maybe you'll get lucky."

Lizzie didn't need that kind of luck. She also didn't need a man. Except for one, and that was an implausible dream. Two months had passed without a word from Jack. Too long to believe that she would ever see him again. "Anything else I can do, Penney?" Sweep the floor? Wash your car?

"That's it. Have fun."

Oh, yeah, lots of fun, Lizzie thought as she trudged to the rear of the salon past the stylists and clients chatting about everything under the sun. The noise droned on like a high-pitched drill, adding irritated eardrums to Lizzie's list of physical aches and pains.

At least the tips were good, but Lizzie wasn't sure how much more abuse her body could take, especially her feet that she'd unwisely dressed in moderate pumps today. Normally she would be solely in charge of makeup and facials but because she needed the extra money, she'd resorted to doing hair again. A lot of hair. And if this guy was even the least bit particular, she'd be tempted to give him a buzz cut whether he wanted one or not.

After reaching the shampoo room, Lizzie found the lone man sitting on a chair in the corner, one navy slack–covered leg crossed over the other—his feet sporting expensive loafers—a white terry towel draped over his head and face. He obviously didn't want water dripping on his precious jacket, the drip. Either that or he *was* a weirdo who wanted to play hide-and-seek with the stylist. If he grabbed her fanny, she would be forced to slap him. For all of womankind, of course.

Lizzie cocked a hip against the door frame and studied her newly polished nails. "I'm ready for you now, sir."

"I certainly hope so, Dorothy."

If Lizzie didn't have the wall to hold her up, she would have collapsed onto the checkerboard tile at the sound of his deep voice.

He slowly removed the towel, revealing his smile, his gorgeous silver eyes and his damp hair that wasn't at all in need of a trim.

Stunned, Lizzie could only gape at Jack even though she wanted to launch herself into his lap. Since their parting, she'd thought about him at least a hundred times a day. And now here he was, in the flesh, but why? And where was her voice? Obviously taking a swift journey down the drain in the shampoo bowl.

He unfolded from the chair and stood, all six-feet-plus of manly man, bringing with him a familiar scent that churned up memories of sultry nights at sea, cool sheets, soft touches, heady kisses....

"How have you been?" he asked.

Miserable. Alone. Lovesick. "I've been great. How about yourself?"

"I've been okay."

"I'm glad."

With his hands firmly planted in his pockets, he just stood there looking as if he didn't know what to say next. Lizzie couldn't stand the uneasy silence, any silence for that matter, so she said, "It's good to see you, Jack."

"It's good to see you, too." He hesitated for a moment. "And I lied."

"It's not good to see me?"

His smile was wan. "No. I mean yes, it's good to

see you. It's great to see you. I lied when you asked me how I've been.''

''What's wrong?''

''Well, I guess you could say—''

''Excuse me.'' One of the stylists pushed past Lizzie with a client following behind her. Then another pair walked in and suddenly the room seemed very crowded.

Lizzie gestured Jack into the corridor where she faced him again. ''You were saying?''

Just then, a little boy came streaking down the hall and stopped to tug on Lizzie's skirt. ''I gotta pee.''

Lizzie pointed toward the back of the salon. ''Right down there, sweetie. Keep going.'' The boy took off at a dead run and slammed the door behind him.

''Is there someplace else we could talk?'' Jack asked.

''Let's try the break room.'' But the break room was occupied by Penney who held up a slice of gooey pepperoni pizza and regarded Jack with a smarmy smile then said, ''Could I interest you in a piece?''

This would not do, Lizzie thought. ''No thanks, Penney, but you go right ahead.''

After they returned to the hall, Lizzie sighed. ''I'm sorry. It's kind of crazy around here, especially on Saturdays.''

''When's your last appointment for the day?''

''Actually, you're it. I was just heading for home before you showed up.'' And she still didn't know why he was there. "Did you really come in for a cut?"

He forked a hand through his hair. "No. I have something I need to show you, if you have the time."

"Where is it?" Whatever *it* was.

"We have to take a drive."

Lizzie nibbled her bottom lip. She wanted to go with him. Truly she did, but her composure had scattered like a deck of dropped cards the moment she'd laid eyes on him. When he left again, that would only serve to deal her heart a world of hurt. "I don't know, Jack. Maybe that's not such a good idea."

He sighed. "Look, I think it will be worth your while."

She would be totally nuts to agree. Wasn't the first time where Jack was concerned. And after all, she had told him to contact her if he needed a friend. Right now he looked as if that's exactly what he needed.

She could be his friend for the day, even if she did want so much more.

"Okay, I'm going to trust you on this one, Ahab."

He sent her a satisfied smile. "I promise you won't be sorry, Dorothy."

Eleven

—

Lizzie wasn't exactly sorry, but she was a little frustrated by the time they pulled through the gate of Miami's ultraexclusive Sky Bridge Yacht Club and Resort located on the Intracoastal Waterway. Jack hadn't said much of anything during the twenty-minute drive, only that he'd been busy for the past few weeks traveling to his hotels throughout the world. Tough break, Lizzie thought with a good deal of sarcasm. The highlight of her life for the past few weeks had involved literal highlights.

And even more exasperating, Jack hadn't even hinted at why they'd come to this particular place. But more important, he hadn't said that he'd missed her.

Even if it hurt like a hornet sting, it really didn't matter. She would graciously take a look at what he had to show her and then she would return to her life with the request that he not bother her again. She couldn't be just a friend. If she wanted to stay on track she didn't need him showing up and reminding her of what she could never have—a future with him in it.

After they pulled into a parking space, Jack turned off the Mercedes's ignition. "We're here."

"Good. Now what do you want to show me?"

He shrugged off his jacket and rolled up his sleeves but still looked very uncomfortable. "I have something to give you before we get out."

"Okay."

He fished in his pocket, withdrew a burgundy velvet jewel box and handed it to her.

Lizzie's heart danced a jig—until she opened it. Now her feelings were caught in a tangled web of joy mixed with disappointment as she stared at the necklace—her necklace—the one she'd thought she'd lost forever. Although she was thrilled to have it back, for one brief moment—one crazy instant— she'd imagined finding a ring inside. An engagement ring. How stupid was that?

Trying to affect enthusiasm, Lizzie smiled as she took the necklace from the box and dangled it from her fingers. "Oh, Jack. I can't believe this. Where did you find it?"

"Actually, the smugglers found it on deck. I forgot to tell you during all the chaos. The police confiscated it and returned it to the hotel a few days ago, so I decided to return it to you in person."

"I'm so glad to have it back." And she was. She'd greatly missed her lucky charms and the good memories of her parents they had so often provided.

When she circled the chain around her neck, Jack said, "Turn around and I'll fasten it."

Lizzie complied and held her hair up, allowing him better access. As he worked the clasp, his fingers brushed against her nape, spreading a warm glow throughout her being. But Lizzie acknowledged it was only common courtesy that prompted his touch, nothing more.

After he had the necklace secured, Lizzie called up her self-control and shifted in the seat to face him again. "So that's what you wanted to show me? My necklace?"

"If that were true, I wouldn't have driven all the way here."

Jack slid out and rounded to Lizzie's side then opened the door for her. She took the hand he offered, immediately jolted by the feel of his callused palm enfolding hers, and even more surprised when he didn't let her go. She realized how very much she had missed touching him, missed everything about him, in fact. But she couldn't let holding hands turn her head. Most likely he worried she might slip and tumble arse over appetite considering her inherent lack of grace while wearing moderate heels.

Jack led Lizzie at a fast clip past the yacht club's luxury condos and onto the boardwalk. Power walking was not one of Lizzie's fave activities even when her feet didn't ache. She wanted to tell him to slow the heck down before she gave in to the urge to scream out from pain as they strode past myriad boats positioned in double rows of slips. They turned left at the end of the L-shaped pier, traveled a few more yards where Jack abruptly stopped before a three-level yacht moored horizontally on the bayside.

A monstrous yacht, at least seventy feet long, that could best be described as a mini cruise ship.

After releasing Lizzie's hand—much to her disappointment—Jack faced her and said, "Well?"

"Well what?"

"How do you like it?"

Lizzie studied the massive streamlined boat gleaming white in the sun hovering over Biscayne Bay. "What's not to like? It's great. A regular traveling hotel. Whose is it?"

He grinned. "Mine. I bought it this morning. Sort of a spontaneous decision."

Lizzie's idea of spontaneity involved chocolate-covered cherry ice cream after dinner. And most of the men she knew bought power tools on a whim, not power yachts. "You bought it just like that?"

"Yeah. A broker called me yesterday and told me about it. It's a one-owner custom. The best cruiser money can buy."

Okay, so now she knew. He'd come to Miami to purchase an extravagant boat and since he was in town anyway, decided to return the necklace in person. Lizzie's disappointment came out in a crabby, "It doesn't have any sails."

"No, it doesn't. Completely motorized with all the amenities. Just wait until you see inside."

Lizzie didn't want to see inside. She didn't want to fall in love with the boat any more than she had wanted to fall in love with the boat's captain, only to discover that both were unattainable. Here today, gone tomorrow.

But Jack was obviously determined to show her whether she wanted it or not. Taking her by the hand again, he led her to an access gate at the stern and on to a door that opened into the main deck. They entered a very grand salon—all elegant refinement, from the lengthy white sofa to the polished teakwood cabinets in the circular galley. Large windows gave the cabin a sense of openness; accent colors of coral and lime lent a Caribbean feel. And darn it all, if Lizzie didn't immediately fall in love with the flat-screen TV suspended from the wall opposite the sofa.

Jack paced the length of the salon while Lizzie strolled around the area, touching the opulent furniture with disbelief. She couldn't begin to imagine the size of the price tag for this house-size boat. She didn't even want to imagine it.

Pointing to the staircase winding upward, she asked, "Where does that go? To the moon?"

"To the flybridge. It has a large deck specifically for sunbathing, with or without the benefit of clothes." Jack's husky voice incited a riot within Lizzie, but not enough of one to tear down her guard or completely dissolve her resistance.

"Great. I guess poor *Hannah* has been thrown over for a better model."

"I still have her. But this boat is much bigger and offers more protection from the elements." He indicated the front of the cabin and another set of stairs leading downward. "Down below there's a guest cabin with twin beds and a master cabin. Three heads total. Overall, there's plenty of room for—"

"A large gathering of socialites?"

"For a family."

Lizzie almost stopped dead on that comment but instead decided to pay it little mind. Decided to ignore the flicker of hope trying to break through. She had no cause to wish or even slightly assume that Jack had meant anything by it.

She faced him again, propelled by an anger she couldn't quite explain. "Very impressive, Jack. I'm happy for you and your new plaything. You know what they say about men and their toys."

"That's not why I bought it, Liz."

How dare he call her Liz. How dare he look at her as if she meant something to him. "Are you sure, Jack? Isn't this just a means to fill that void in your life? That's all well and good, but can possessions really do that?"

"No, they can't. And no one realizes that better than me, especially now."

Lizzie propped her hands on her hips. "Then why buy it? Unless you intend to go into the chartering business. But I can't imagine why you'd do that. You obviously don't need the money."

"You're right, I don't need any money. But I do need you."

Surely he hadn't said…no, she must've heard wrong. "Excuse me?"

"You heard me. I need you. The rest of it doesn't matter, all of the money and prestige. Not without you to share in it."

This time he took both her hands and guided her to the sofa. They sat side by side while Lizzie tried to clear the mental haze away by counting the glasses housed in the built-in bar's display case opposite them. Those were real; this whole scenario was surreal.

"Lizzie, look at me." She did and found Jack sporting a soulful expression that went straight to the heart. "I tried to go back to business as usual. When that didn't work, I took Hannah back out to sea expecting to return to my life the way it was before I met you. I couldn't.''

Hope came barreling in and ran right over her caution. ''You couldn't?''

''No. But the solitude turned out to be a good thing this time. I got my head on straight and made a few decisions.''

''What decisions?''

''I decided I don't want to be Hank's godfather.''

Any hope Lizzie had entertained fell with a heavy thud on her soul. ''That's okay. I understand. You don't have to—''

''I want to be his father. I want to be a part of his life, your life, if you'll have me.''

Lizzie drew in a deep breath and released it slowly. ''I'm not sure I'm following you, Jack.''

He inched a little closer. ''When I went to the salon today, I stood outside for a long time because I wasn't sure what I was going to say to you. Then I left.''

Now she was really confused. ''Left?''

''Yeah. I went out and bought something else.'' He released her hands and dug into his pocket again, this time withdrawing a blue velvet box that he opened in his large palm. ''I probably should have let you pick it out, but this one caught my eye. I hope it's okay.''

Okay? *Okay* didn't come close to describing the huge emerald-cut diamond ring centered on a baguette-encrusted band. Lizzie couldn't do anything but stare, her lips parting in response to her shock.

''Will you marry me, Elizabeth Matheson?''

Lizzie's gaze zipped from the ring to Jack's silver eyes. "Marry you?"

"Yeah."

"Marry you?"

"I didn't realize this place echoed so badly."

Lizzie wanted to blurt out, "Yes!" She wanted to dance and sing and kiss the fool out of him. But first she had to know exactly why he'd proposed because otherwise she might be a fool to accept. After all, he hadn't said a thing about love. "Jack, if you're doing this because of Hank, I promise we'll be fine. I can make a good life for him. I won't be alone anymore."

He pulled the ring from the holder then set the box on the table before them. "I'm doing this because I can't stand the thought of not having you in my life to give me grief on a daily basis." He leaned over and brushed a kiss on her cheek. "And more important, I'm doing this because I love you."

Oh my gosh, he loved her? "Are you sure, Jack?"

"Never been more sure of anything in my life."

"Even if I am high-maintenance, I think you called it and—"

"Lizzie—"

"Let's face it, it's a big responsibility, taking on a wife and a baby—"

"Lizzie—"

"Plus, I still don't eat meat—"

"Lizzie."

"What?"

"You told me the day you left that you loved me. I hope to God that you still do, but I understand why you wouldn't after the way I've treated you."

"Treated me?" Tears burned hot behind her eyes

and she fought with every fiber of her being to keep them tucked away. "You've been wonderful to me. You took care of me and protected me. You saved my life."

"You saved mine."

She flipped a hand in dismissal. "I picked up a trophy and whacked a thief on the head with it. Anyone would've done that."

"I didn't mean that night with the smugglers, although you did save my life then, too. I meant you've saved me from a totally worthless existence. Made me realize how much I've been missing by not having someone in it. But not just anyone. You." He surveyed her eyes for a long, meaningful moment. "Do you still love me?"

How could she deny it? She couldn't. "I do. I really thought I could stop but I knew that wasn't going to happen when you showed up today."

He caught her left hand and held it up, the ring poised at the tip of her finger. "Then would you do me the honor of being my life partner?"

This was no time to be rendered mute, but she was.

Jack frowned. "It's a simple yes-or-no question, Lizzie. I've never known you to be without some kind of response."

She tried to look serious when all she wanted to do was shout out the happiness she felt inside. "You could have gone all day without pointing that out."

"It's one of the many things I love about you, Liz."

She looked into his eyes so full of promise and saw her future there. Hers and Hank's future. And the word that had eluded her to that point slipped out on a breathy sigh. "Yes."

Jack slid the ring on her finger, a near-perfect fit, then said, "Good. Now shut up and kiss me."

Jack's lips met hers, warm and inviting, in a kiss that was tender in the beginning but turned onto a reckless course, heading straight for a passionate curve. His palm settled on her breast and Lizzie's hand landed on his thigh. One more pass over her needy flesh, one more sensuous stroke of his tongue, and she was taking him down on the sofa.

Much to Lizzie's dismay, Jack ended the kiss, dropped his hand and tipped his forehead against hers. "I'm sorry. I don't want you to think that this is only about sex."

"I'm not sorry at all. I've recently discovered how fond I am of sex, thanks to you."

Jack pulled her up from the sofa. "I have one more thing to show you."

"J.J.?"

His grin knocked the wind out of her sails. "Eventually."

"The bedroom?"

He rubbed his chin, looking thoughtful and drop-dead handsome. "That's right. We haven't seen that cabin yet."

Lizzie circled her arms around his waist. "I'm ready when you are."

"I'm more than ready, after we go outside."

Outside? "You want to do it outside?"

"A novel idea, but I have something else to show you. First, you have to close your eyes."

"But Jack—"

He popped a kiss on her mouth. "I promise you'll like it."

Lizzie had no idea how Jack could possibly top

the return of her necklace, the gorgeous ring, the proposal and especially his admission of love. But she decided to trust him once more as he led her into the sunlight, urging her to keep her eyes closed for a few more minutes, a few more steps.

Taking her by the shoulders, he turned her around and said, "Okay, you can look now."

Lizzie opened her eyes to find they had moved back onto the dock and stood at the back of the boat. "What am I supposed to be seeing?"

"Look below the swim deck," he whispered, his palms planted firmly on her shoulders.

Lizzie finally cleared away the confusion when she noted the name emblazoned in black letters across the boat. Her name.

The *Lizzie*.

She turned to Jack and hugged his neck hard, barely able to contain her excitement. "I've never had anyone name anything after me before."

Jack looked a little uneasy. "Actually, it was already named. When I got the call from the broker, I had no intention of buying another boat, much less a cruiser. But then he called it the *Lizzie* and said it was in Miami. I had to believe that this was destiny, as crazy as it sounds. You and I were meant to be together."

She softly kissed his lips. "I don't think it's crazy at all, Jack. I'm just wondering why it took you so long to figure it out."

"Guess I'm just a little slow on the uptake when it comes to matters of the heart. Regardless of how it turned out, I would have eventually named a boat after you anyway."

"I'm sure you say that to all your girlfriends," Lizzie teased.

"I guarantee I've never named a boat after a girlfriend."

"The *Hannah*?"

"That's my mother's name."

Lizzie touched his face in reaction to the sadness in his eyes. "I'm sorry, Jack. I guess you miss your folks as much as I miss mine."

"Yeah, but we'll have our own family now. You and me and Hank."

"Shall we take *Lizzie* out for a spin?"

"Not until we have a proper christening with champagne. And since we don't have any champagne at the moment, I guess we'll just have to initiate the boat our own way while she's docked."

"And how do you propose we do that, Captain?"

He winked. "Let's go inside and I'll let J.J. show you."

"That sounds great if my poor tormented feet will get me back to the boat."

"We can certainly remedy that." Jack hauled Lizzie into his arms and carried her toward the boat.

When they arrived at the aft entrance, Lizzie said, "Put me down a sec." She strode to the railing, yanked off her shoes, threw them overboard then turned and brushed her palms together. "I just couldn't stand those heels any longer."

Sporting a wicked smile, Jack leaned back against the door. "Anything else you care to take off and discard?"

Lizzie looked around and finding the immediate area deserted, said, "You betcha." She worked her straps down her arms and slipped her bra from be-

neath her sleeveless blouse, then hurled it like a
slingshot into the bay. "How's that?"

Jack crossed his arms over his chest, his eyes reflecting a heat she'd definitely seen before, several
times in fact. "Don't stop now. You're doing great."

"You are so bad, Ahab."

"And you are so good, Dorothy."

Lizzie lifted her skirt, shimmied out of her panties
then tossed them into the water to join her shoes and
bra. "Anything else?"

He slowly looked her up and down. "I'm thinking."

She sent a pointed look at his fly. "Well, shiver
me timbers, Ahab—and my timbers are shivering, by
the way—but I do believe J.J. has a few ideas of his
own."

He grinned. "What am I going to do with you for
the next fifty years?"

"You're going to have a great time. But right now
I'm more concerned with what you plan to do with
me once we get back inside. I could really use a good
ravishing about now."

Jack raised an eyebrow. "Who said anything about
waiting until we get back inside?"

Lizzie pointed a finger at him. "Okay, who are
you and what have you done with cautious Captain
Jack?"

"Let's just say I'm throwing all caution to the
wind."

"Oh, I like the way that sounds."

"Good. Now come here."

Like the obedient child she had never been, Lizzie
answered Jack's command and immediately discovered that her amenable behavior paid off. Jack

whirled her around and backed her up against the door recessed between two shallow walls, their only protection from meddling eyes. He kissed her thoroughly while she worked the buttons open on his tailored white shirt, parting the fabric so she could run her hands over that luscious male terrain.

He left her lips to whisper, "You have no idea how much I've thought about this over the past two months."

"Oh yes I do," Lizzie said. "And after the baby's born, I intend to get you on a balloon so we can make love in midair."

He slid one palm to the front of her thigh, just beneath the hem of her skirt. "I'm not so sure about that, Dorothy."

"You'll love it once you're airborne. It's the closest to heaven you'll ever be."

"I disagree." He buried his face in her neck, calling up some mighty nice chills down Lizzie's spine. "Making love to you anywhere qualifies."

No one had ever said anything so sweet to Lizzie before. But then she'd never met a man like Jack Dunlap. "Then what are we waiting for?"

"Not a thing."

With that, Jack slipped his hand completely beneath her skirt and found just the right spot, almost bringing Lizzie to her knees.

"You are definitely primed for action," Jack said as he plied her with silken strokes.

"Oh, yeah," she said, the only thing she could manage in light of Jack's wild and wicked foreplay, right there in the daylight where anyone who decided to pass by could see.

Someone whistled and Jack took his hand away.

"We better go inside. I'm not taking any chances that someone might call the harbor patrol and subsequently land us in jail."

The thought of spending one minute without Jack didn't sit well with Lizzie. "You're right. Inside it is."

"And inside I will soon be." Again he swept her up into his strong arms where she could feel his heart beating in a rapid rhythm that matched her own.

"Come to think of it, I'm not too thrilled to think that some sailor is going to have your underwear for his collection," he said as he carried her into the salon.

"It could be worse. We could wake up tomorrow morning to a headline that reads, 'Dolphin Found Sporting Women's Lingerie on Snout.'"

Jack laughed, a musical sound that made Lizzie laugh, too. But she stopped laughing when Jack halted and slid her down the length of him, letting her know up-front what he intended. He kissed her deeply, deliberately, sending her pulse on a sprint and a fiery heat spiraling throughout her body.

Once they parted, he said, "Could I show you to the rest of the accommodations now, Dorothy?"

"'Bout time, Ahab."

They hurried down the steps to the deck below, pausing for more kisses while leaving a trail of clothing on the journey to the master cabin. Lizzie didn't have the opportunity to really study the area since Jack had her stretched out on the bed before she had time to blink. But she did know that the sheets beneath her back were satin and the lights above her head, recessed into the ceiling.

After turning onto his side, Jack smoothed a palm

over her breasts before moving down to her rounded belly. But when he lingered there, with his hand and his gaze, Lizzie felt somewhat self-conscious. "I've gained a little weight since the last time we were together," she said.

He planted a kiss on her abdomen and murmured, "You're beautiful just the way you are."

Funny, she really did feel beautiful. She also felt totally lost as Jack alternated between using his skilled mouth and his equally skilled hands in intimate places, sending her precariously close to the edge. Lizzie could barely draw a breath, barely think by the time Jack kissed his way back up her torso and settled his lips on her breasts. She focused on him then, reaching out to touch and explore with provocative, purposeful strokes just so she could see the desire burning bright in his eyes.

"You're incredible," she murmured as she skimmed a fingertip up and down the length of him.

"It's all for you, babe." He moved above her and slid inside her with a slow, tempered glide. "Only for you."

And he gave her his all, drawing her into paradise little by little with every stroke, every rhythmic motion of his powerful body.

Don't be over, Lizzie mentally chanted as the pleasant pressure continued to build. Not now, not yet....

But her silent pleas went unheeded as the climax overpowered her, claimed her with a heavenly assault. Jack's body went rigid in her arms, all tensile muscle and taut, masculine flesh as his own release took hold, filtering out in a hiss of breath and the sound of her name.

With the exception of their ragged respiration, the cabin was cloaked in silence—a comfortable, calming silence that Lizzie cherished with every rapid beat of her heart. But not as much as she cherished the man in her arms.

Jack lifted his head and smiled. "I love you, Liz."

"How much?"

"More than I ever expected to love anyone."

"Good, because I have a request."

He frowned. "If you're thinking that I'm going to become a vegetarian after we get married—"

"That's not it." She kissed his chin. "But it is about our marriage. The wedding, actually."

"What about it?"

"I happen to know the perfect place..."

Jack couldn't believe he'd agreed to this, but Lizzie had a way of talking him into things he'd never imagined doing. He hadn't intended to fall in love with her, sure as hell hadn't intended to settle down and never in his wildest daredevil fantasies had he ever considered getting married while suspended above the earth.

But here they were—Lizzie, a fellow pilot named Grady, a rotund minister who also happened to be a balloonist, and Jack—all crowded into a wicker basket for the official ceremony.

Lizzie had never looked more beautiful to Jack even though she had worried over her wardrobe because her pregnancy had become more apparent with each passing day. But the white lace dress she had chosen—after dragging Jack to at least twenty bridal boutiques—only enhanced her finer features, including her breasts that had become much fuller over the past month, much to Lizzie's delight. Jack certainly hadn't complained although he loved everything about her. And he personally couldn't wait to take the dress off of her tonight—as soon as they were back on solid ground, or solid ocean, as the case might be since they were setting out on the *Lizzie* later tonight for their honeymoon. No ringing phones, no business to attend to, only time to be together—and a whole lot of lovemaking.

A mild breeze ruffled Lizzie's golden hair and the sun reflected in her blue-green eyes. She sent him a smile as the balloon ascended into the cloudless sky, only the sound of the burner disturbing the serenity.

Jack focused on Lizzie's eyes, not the disappearing ground. He held her hand although he had the urge to grab the side of the damn basket. But amazingly enough, the movement was barely discernible, as if they were almost standing still.

Lizzie leaned over and whispered, "You look nervous. Are you having second thoughts?"

He brushed a kiss across her cheek. "Not hardly. I thought today would never get here."

She studied him a long moment. "You aren't afraid of heights, are you?"

"Let's just say I'm not that fond of traveling thousands of feet from the ground in a flimsy basket."

"Jack, it's only a hundred feet up, we're tethered to the ground and if you recall, my basket gave your boat a run for its money, so I think it will hold us for the next fifteen minutes or so."

"You're right. But a nice wedding chapel would have worked."

"I personally think this is a perfect place for a

wedding. I mean, if you did change your mind, you couldn't go anywhere.''

''Believe me, Liz, I'm not going anywhere.''

Once they reached the end of the line, the minister said, ''Are we ready to begin?''

Lizzie faced Jack. ''Are you ready?''

''Definitely.''

Jack and Lizzie exchanged traditional vows and their rings, but when it was time to kiss the bride to seal the deal—the part Jack had looked forward to most—Lizzie pressed a finger to his lips and regarded the minister. ''Excuse me, Reverend Michaels. I have a few more things to ask my husband.''

The minister smiled. ''Be my guest.''

She met Jack's gaze. ''Do you promise to try tofu at least once?''

''If I must.''

''And do you promise to discuss any major purchases with me from this point forward? Not that I minded the new boat. I mean, who would mind that?''

She was absolutely priceless, Jack thought. ''I promise. Anything else?''

''Yes. Do you promise to take Hank, for better or for worse, through midnight feedings and dirty diapers?''

''You bet.''

''Okay, now you may kiss the bride.''

''Thank God.''

Jack leaned over and kissed Lizzie with all the love for her that lived deep within his healing soul. Lizzie wrapped her arms around his waist and Jack suddenly forgot where they were when the world seemed to fall away, just as Lizzie had said it would.

Jack finally ended the kiss when he realized they were slowly descending.

The minister cleared his throat. "I will now recite the balloonist's prayer as you begin your life together. The winds have welcomed you with softness. The sun has blessed you with warm hands. You have flown so high and so well, that God has joined you in your laughter and has set you gently back into the loving arms of Mother Earth."

With that, the basket landed in the capable hands of Grady and was secured by Lizzie's crew. They were greeted with applause and cheers from the onlookers surrounding the platform—a large group of Lizzie's friends and Jack's colleagues, all prepared for a grand reception to follow at the Key Largo resort.

Jack didn't mind throwing a party; in fact, he had been more than happy to do it. But he intended to leave early so he could get his wife alone and divested of her clothes.

When the minister and pilot exited the basket, Jack pulled Lizzie close to his heart. "You know something?"

"What?"

"For the first time in a long time, I feel like a damn lucky man."

Lizzie toyed with the necklace resting between her breasts. "I'm pretty lucky, too. And so is my son, considering he's going to have such a wonderful father."

Jack brushed her hair away and rested a palm on the place that sheltered their unborn child. "That's our son, Lizzie. Our little boy."

Epilogue

Jack studied the little girl in his arms, so fragile and innocent with her ocean-blue eyes and downy blond hair, a miniature version of her mother. He'd never paid much attention to babies before now, but he couldn't seem to quit marveling over this one. But then she was *his* child, all his, regardless of her biological beginnings.

Lizzie left the hospital bed where she'd been packing for their return home—a home they had bought together a week following their month-long honeymoon. A two-story house with a huge backyard and a dog named Lucky that Lizzie had rescued from the pound, just as she had rescued Jack from a life not worth living.

Coming to Jack's side, Lizzie laid a hand on the baby's cheek. "I still can't believe she's a girl."

"I still can't believe we don't have a name."

Lizzie sighed. "I know, but I just can't make Henrietta work. I do have a suggestion."

"Bessie?"

"Hannah."

Jack couldn't think of anything he would like more. "You're right. Hannah it is. My mother would have loved that."

"And my mother's name was Caroline, so I'd like that to be her middle name."

"Perfect."

Lizzie gave him a perfect smile. "You can put her down in the crib until they discharge me."

"I could, but I really don't want to."

"Oh, heavens, you're going to spoil her rotten just like you've spoiled me."

Jack kissed Lizzie's cheek. "And what's wrong with that?"

"Well, nothing, I guess, but I want her to appreciate the value of life, not necessarily things."

"We'll teach her that."

"Okay, we'll do that. And while we're talking about the future, I still have to get you up in a balloon for a real ride."

"Funny you should mention that." Jack strolled toward the window with Hannah resting on his shoulder in peaceful slumber. "Come here for a minute."

"Why?"

"I have something to show you."

She sighed. "Jack, you always have something to show me."

"True, and if I hadn't shown you something the other night, Hannah might have been two weeks late instead of one."

Lizzie grinned. "And what a way to begin labor."

Jack handed the baby to Lizzie and opened the shade to reveal the hospital parking lot—and the gift he'd been waiting to give her for months. Waited until exactly the right time, and that would definitely be now from the astonished look on Lizzie's face. She glowed from the inside out.

"Oh my gosh, Jack! When did you do this?"

He surveyed the bright purple-and-sun-yellow balloon inflated on the lot with Lizzie's former chase crew standing nearby, giving them a thumbs-up. "I've been planning it for a while now. It took some time to have the envelope made since it's a custom job."

Lizzie giggled. "I kind of figured that. I really doubt you'll find another that says Dorothy and Ahab."

Jack moved behind his wife, his soul mate, his savior, and slipped his arms around her waist.

Lizzie leaned back against him. "When Hannah's a little older, I want to take her up for her first flight."

"I'll teach her how to sail."

"And I'll teach her how to fly. I intend to teach you, too."

"You already have, Liz, without the benefit of a balloon." He kissed her neck and held her tighter. "And you know something else?"

She looked back at him, love shining in her eyes. "You have another surprise?"

"No, only something I need to say." He kissed her gently, with gratitude, acknowledging that she had brought him that elusive peace. "No matter how this all turned out—and it's turned out damn good—I would have loved you anyway."

*   *   *   *   *

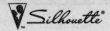

COMING NEXT MONTH

#1519 SCENES OF PASSION—Suzanne Brockmann
Maggie Stanton knew something was missing from her picture-perfect life, and when she ran into her high school buddy Michael Stone, she knew just what it was. The former bad boy had grown into a charismatic man who was everything Maggie had ever dreamed of. But if they were to have a future together, Maggie would have to learn to trust him.

#1520 CINDERELLA'S MILLIONAIRE—Katherine Garbera
Dynasties: The Barones
Love was the last thing on widower Joseph Barone's mind…until he was roped into escorting pastry chef Holly Fitzgerald to a media interview. The brooding millionaire had built an impenetrable wall around his heart, but delectable Holly was pure temptation. He needed her—in his bed and in his life—but was he ready to risk his heart again?

#1521 IN BED WITH THE ENEMY—Kathie DeNosky
Lone Star Country Club
ATF agent Cole Yardley didn't believe women belonged in the field, fighting crime, but then a gun-smuggling investigation brought him and FBI agent Elise Campbell together. Though he'd intended to ignore Elise, Cole soon found himself surrendering to the insatiable hunger she stirred in him.…

#1522 EXPECTING THE COWBOY'S BABY—Charlene Sands
An old flame came roaring back to life when Cassie Munroe went home for her brother's wedding and ran into Jake Griffin, her high school ex. The boy who'd broken her heart was gone, and in his place was one sinfully sexy man. They wound up sharing an unforgettable night of passion that would change Cassie's life forever, for now she was pregnant with Jake's baby!

#1523 CHEROKEE DAD—Sheri WhiteFeather
Desperate to keep her nephew safe, Heather Richmond turned to Michael Elk, the man she'd left behind eighteen months ago. Michael still touched her soul in a way no other man ever had, and she couldn't resist the seductive promises in his eyes. She only hoped he would forgive her once he discovered her secret.…

#1524 THE GENTRYS: CAL—Linda Conrad
When Cal Gentry went home to his family ranch to recover from the accident that killed his wife, he found Isabella de la Cruz on his doorstep. ~~The~~ mysterious beauty needed protecting…and soon found a sense of ~~in~~ Cal's arms. Then, as things heated up between them, Cal ~~convince~~ Isabella to accept not only his protection, but his

SDCNM0603